Manto

SELECTED STORIES

Translated by Aatish Taseer

RANDOM HOUSE INDIA

Published by Random House India in 2008
2468109753

Copyright © Estate of Saadat Hasan Manto
Translation and introduction copyright © Aatish Taseer 2008

Random House Publishers India Private Limited
MindMill Corporate Tower,
2nd Floor, Plot No 24A,
Sector 16A, Noida 201301, UP

Random House Group Limited
20 Vauxhall Bridge Road
London SW1V 2SA
United Kingdom

ISBN 978 81 8400 049 8

Printed and bound in India by Replika Press Private Limited

For Zafar Moradabadi,
and in memory of my grandfather
Dr MD Taseer

Contents

Introduction

Travellers of the Last Night[*]

When at the age of twenty one, I went to Lahore to meet my Pakistani father for the first time in my adult life, I was given, in addition to a new Pakistani family, a copy of my grandfather's poems. It was a blue book, simply published, with flames dancing on the cover. Those flames stood for aatish, fire in Urdu, because the book's title—and the origin of my name—was aatish kada, fire temple. This picture of the flames was all I could make sense of at the time—the poems were in the Urdu script, of which I knew too little to read even my name. My grandfather had died in 1950 when my father was only six. This book then, both for being my only patrimony and for being written in a script I couldn't read, was a mysterious gift.

But deeper than these particular circumstances was another mystery: the mystery of why the script should have been unfamiliar to me at all. My mother's family were Sikhs from what is today Pakistani Punjab; they would have lived no more than a few hundred kilometres from where my father's family lived; they would have spoken the same languages, namely Punjabi and some Urdu. They came, in 1947, as refugees to Delhi, which along with Lucknow, was the centre of Urdu. So how was it that I, six decades later, having grown up in Delhi, could not read my paternal grandfather's poems?

---

[*] Loosely derived from Faiz Ahmed Faiz's poem, 'Sham-e-Firaq'

'They stole it! And we also let it go,' Zafar Morada-badi said mournfully, speaking of Pakistan and Urdu respectively. He was the man with whom I had sat down, four years after receiving my strange patrimony, to conquer its mysteries.

He came to me through the Ghalib Academy, a crumbling, art deco building with pink walls and smelly carpets. Himself a poet, Zafar's name twice resonated the names of poets before him: Zafar like the poet-king, Bahadur Shah Zafar; Moradabadi, like Jigar Moradabadi, the other, more famous, product of the brass producing town of Moradabad.

Zafar didn't like coming to me through the Academy. I felt he was embarrassed at having to teach. Even on the telephone, he seemed to want to establish a reason other than need for teaching me.

'Aatish? Aatish Taseer?' he asked in his papery voice, 'But that's a poet's name.'

'Yes, sir. My grandfather was a poet. I want to learn to read his poetry.'

'Your grandfather was MD Taseer, the poet, and you don't know Urdu?'

'Yes.'

'Then it appears I have something of a duty to teach you.'

He came to see me a few days later. He had a light, gliding step. He wore a safari suit, a white woollen cap and finely made spectacles. He was of medium height with a slight stoop. His eyes were yellow, his skin dark, he had a pencil thin moustache and sores, black and bleeding, ate away at his scalp.

I saw them when I asked if he would like to take his cap off.

'I wear it because the wool from my head has come off,' he said, and laughed throatily. Then, folding away his cap, he revealed his bald head.

'I can't take the heat,' he apologised, when he saw me notice the sores.

He sat there with his hands discreetly by his side. He asked no prying questions, he didn't look around the flat. I asked him if he would like tea.

'I don't normally. My constitution is quite sensitive.'

We started badly. I said I didn't want to learn to write, only to read.

'You can't take a language, break it into pieces, take what you like and leave the rest for the Pakistanis. What if you find you need to write?'

'But I always write on my computer.'

'Yes, but what if you're in a poetry reading and you want to scribble down a couplet.'

'I can write it in Devanagari.'

His face filled with placid disgust.

'Then perhaps you should learn Hindi.'

'My grandfather's poetry…'

'I could have it transcribed for you in Devanagari. Problem solved.'

'Listen, please, I want to read Faiz, Manto, Chughtai…'

'All available in Devanagari.'

'I'll learn to write.'

His face bloomed with affection and concern. 'You know you have a responsibility. You're a poet's grandson; your great-uncle was Faiz; you have a tradition to uphold.

I'm not saying that you should write poetry. I would never send you into poetry. It's finished. Look at how I've suffered. I tell my children all the time that poetry is finished. But what's been done is still there, for you to read and know. You say you want just to read; even that will only come when you can write.'

I offered tea again. He said he didn't normally drink it, but he would today.

When Sati came in with the tea a few minutes later, Zafar was saying in Urdu that life had forced him to become an intellectual mercenary. Those two words, neither of which I knew, provided us with our first thrill as teacher and student. We stumbled about for a bit, coming up with mental soldier, then I was sure I had it. 'Think tank!' We backtracked and gave up. It was only when he explained further that I understood what he had meant.

'I gave birth,' he said, 'to seven PhDs before I was born, and since my own birth, I have given birth to two more. It's dishonest, I know. I take money to write people's theses for them, undeserving people. It's wrong, I know. But I only ever did it from need. I feel that makes it less wrong.'

'How did you start doing it?'

'I used to work as an accountant,' he replied, 'but that slipped away from me. The accounts were computerised. I needed money badly. I even had a breakdown, you know?'

'What kind of breakdown?'

'A nervous breakdown. I was lucky—a south Indian doctor helped me. Only he knew what it was. Without him, I wouldn't be here today. There was a threat of my brain haemorrhaging.'

'Can that happen from a nervous breakdown?'

'Yes, my head used to become so hot, my wife couldn't touch it.'

I began to think of his sores differently.

'He used to tell me, "You have to stop thinking." I said, "Doctor saab, it is my nature. Can you order a flower to stop giving off its scent? It is God given." '

He shook lightly with inaudible laughter, finishing in a wheeze.

'At that point,' he said, 'a PhD candidate came to me. He had a famously strict advisor. A man who used to tear up theses if he didn't like them. He asked me to help him. I said, "Listen, I can't do this. I haven't done your research. I don't know what you wish to say." But, he went away and came back with all his books, begging me. I said, "Let's just try it. If he likes it, then we'll continue." He agreed and I wrote the thesis.'

'Did the professor like it?'

'He said it was the best thing he'd read in twenty years of advising. After that, word spread,' he added bitterly. 'Would you like a cigarette?'

'Yes,' I replied though I wasn't really a smoker, 'but outside.'

We smoked a Win cigarette on the balcony. There, overlooking heavy Delhi trees, he brought up money.

'I can't take less than five thousand,' he said, taking back the blue and white packet.

'A month?'

'Yes.'

My face became hot with shame, but I said nothing. Neither his sores nor his haggard face could have expressed his poverty more extremely. He wanted five thousand rupees for two–three hours, five days a week. I had just paid twice that amount at Barbarian gym. I didn't know how to say I wanted to give him more. I didn't want to upset his calculations. So we settled at five thousand a month and Zafar began to come every day to teach me Urdu, from three to six.

Zafar had become a poet and moved to Delhi in the days when it was still possible to do so. Making a living as a poet was never easy, but in the early seventies there was still an Urdu literary culture, there were publishers, there were well attended discussions and readings and most of all, there were still poets. And for many, there was the Bombay screen where men like Sahir Ludhianvi and Shakeel Badayuni, to name only a few, were able to supplement their income as song writers. It was a time when, Zafar recalled, horse carriages would run along the stretch of road that connected the Red Fort to Fatehpuri. The road itself, now treeless, was then lined with many shade-giving trees.

In the four decades that passed, from the time when Zafar moved to Delhi to the time when he started teaching me Urdu, he saw that world, the world in which it was still feasible to be an Urdu poet, die around him. The movies changed, the literary gatherings became fewer and less well attended, Urdu publishing sank, India stopped producing major poets at all, and even the city Zafar had moved to, the city that had nurtured men like Mir, Ghalib, Momin and Dagh, turned to slum. Zafar blamed a part of this decay on what he saw as the artificial claim by Pakistan on Urdu. Urdu was not the natural language of any part of what would become the territory of Pakistan; with its many Persian and Arabic borrowings, it was imported as a way for the new state to realise its Islamic aims; and it was possible to see this as co-opting high culture from one place and transplanting it to another. Zafar knew that Pakistan, as a secular state for Indian Muslims, would have always had to do cultural acrobatics of this kind. What he could less easily forgive was secular India, in response, he felt, Sanskritising Hindi and letting Urdu sink. But Zafar was only half right.

He was the first to admit that Urdu in India hadn't really sunk; its literary culture, like with many Indian languages in the post Independence years, had declined, but as a language, it dominated television and cinema; it was still understood, still spoken. The Indian state had tried, and continues to try, putting forward a Sanskritised Hindi—prompting the actor Johnny Walker to remark, 'They [news broadcasters] should not announce "Ab Hindi mein samachar suniye" [Now, we'll hear the news in Hindi], but "Ab samachar mein Hindi suniye" [Now, we'll hear some Hindi in the news]'—but Bollywood, and later television, put up a far more robust front for the language to remain what it was. And it is that language of Bombay cinema, with its heavy Urdu influence, in which a traveller is a musafir, not a yatri, and a conspiracy, a saazish, not a shadyantra, that endures as the language of undivided north India, understood effortlessly on both sides of the Indian and Pakistani borders. So when I pressed Zafar about what he had meant, he confessed that it was a question of lippi or script: what had stood between me and my grandfather's poetry.

Zafar felt that it would have been possible to retain the Arabic–Persian script for this hybrid language, even after Independence. But the question of script had become heavy with religious and political sentiment—often related to liturgical texts—long before Independence, and I couldn't imagine Hindu majority India accepting the Arabic–Persian script for its main national language. Zafar's own passion for his script was an indicator of corresponding passions in Sikhs and Hindus for theirs. And later, he confessed, using the word mizaaj, which is disposition, temperament and taste, 'One's mizaaj is contained in one's script.'

Zafar's charge that Urdu had been falsely claimed by Pakistan also needed qualification. It was true that Urdu was not the natural language of the land that was to be Pakistan, but a great majority of the demand for the new state, and later the immigration, came from Urdu speaking India. More importantly, Urdu had come as an import to Punjab well before Independence and Punjab, by the early twentieth century, in men like Allama Iqbal and later Faiz Ahmed Faiz, was producing its great modern poets. It was into this flowering of Urdu in Punjab that my grandfather was born in 1902. And it was ten years later, into that still youthful age, when the first war had not yet begun, when Gandhi was still to return to India, when Jallianwala Bagh was just a public garden, that Saadat Hasan Manto was born. By the time he was dead in 1955, only forty two years later, there had been another war, an independence movement and a partition that left Manto in one country and Bombay, the city he wrote most about, in another. He had first gone there as a young man; he worked in its film industry through the thirties and forties; he left for Lahore soon after Partition when Hindu–Muslim violence erupted in the city. Though born in the Ludhiana district, and at times in his life, a resident of Amritsar, Delhi and Lahore, it was Bombay he loved and never got over.

And it was some six months into my lessons with Zafar that, when newly reading in Urdu and hungry for prose, I read my first Manto story about Bombay. The affection that had grown between Zafar and I softened his insistence on teaching me to write. I'd mastered the script's meaningful single and double dots and mysterious elisions, but if I confused the dot for an 'n' with the dot for a 'b', Zafar would croak irritably that if I'd followed his advice and learned to write first, none of this would have been a problem. He brought me an Indian edition of Manto's stories, but it was badly printed and the glue stank. When I sent for a Pakistani edition, he took offence. If ever he found an error in the printing, a crucial dot missing, he'd say, 'The Pakistanis have stolen it.'

The story we began with was 'Ten Rupees'. It is a story about a girl in a Bombay chawl, called Sarita, who is still under fifteen and young for her age when her mother and a procurer called Kishori send her into prostitution. But Sarita is unaware of these circumstances because she is blinded by a great love. Sarita loves cars so much that her dealings with men become just another occasion for her to ride in a motor car, to feel the blasts of wind and to see the trees around her race; she hardly knows she's a prostitute. And this innocence in the foreground, with the squalor of the chawl and Sarita's trade in the background, become the lines on which the story's tension is cast. The narrative is set around a day in the country that Sarita spends with three young clients from Hyderabad.

> In the main market, a yellow car was parked outside a long factory wall, near a small board that read, 'It is forbidden to urinate here.' Inside, the three young Hyderabadi men waiting for Kishori held their handkerchiefs to their noses. They would have liked to park the car ahead somewhere, but the factory wall was long and the stench of urine drifted down its entire stretch.

Sarita appears a few minutes later in a blue georgette sari. There's some initial awkwardness, but as the car picks up speed, her excitement takes over. Soon she and the Hyderabadi boys are driving fast through the countryside, singing Devika Rani and Ashok Kumar songs and composing duets.

> Then the road straightened and the seashore came in sight. The sun was setting and the sea wind brought a chill in the air.
> The car stopped. Sarita opened the door, jumped out and began to run along the shore. Kafayat and Shahab ran behind her. In the open air, on the edge of the vast ocean, with the great palms rising up from the wet sand, Sarita didn't know what it was that she wanted. She wished she could melt into the sky; spread through the ocean; fly so high that she could see the palm canopies from above; for all

the wetness of the shore to seep from the sand into her feet and then… and then for that same racing engine, that same speed, those blasts of wind, the car honking—she was very happy.

This is the climax of 'Ten Rupees': the sudden view of the sea; the chill at close of day; and the abandon of a young prostitute who cannot express her situation. Manto, as if relishing what might seem like an anti-climax, bends the narrative around something as ordinary as a ten rupee note, which Sarita accepts in a moment of excitement from one of the boys, but returns at the end of the story. '"This… why should I take this money?" she replied and ran off, leaving Kafayat still staring at the limp note.'

When I finished 'Ten Rupees', I knew that something about the quality of its detail, and the oblique gaze of the narrator, the story of a chawl and a prostitute told through a girl's love of cars, had altered my life as a reader. If before, I had read looking for language and rhythms that I liked, I was reading now to understand how a writer like Manto could evoke his world with a single detail; I was reading to see how he engaged his material so that a narrative seemed to spring naturally from it, a narrative that not only didn't rely on ornate writing and description, but would have been obscured by it. So affecting was the experience that I wondered why I hadn't grown up reading Manto. The answer, I discovered, was that he wasn't taught widely in schools; and though his language would easily have been understood by the average north Indian reader, he was locked into Urdu curriculums; Devanagari editions of his stories were hard to come by and English translations of his writing dense and bland; he had either been forgotten in India, or disowned. Feeling I knew why, and feeling also that India had too few writers of his calibre—either with the richness and breadth of his material or the simplicity of his prose—to allow any to leave for Pakistan, I sat down to do the first translation of 'Ten Rupees'.

At the time, I was forming my first understanding of economy, an understanding to which Manto was to become essential. Just a few weeks earlier, an older writer friend had suggested I read Pushkin, Gandhi and RK Narayan to see what they did. I had begun with Pushkin, reading first *The Captain's Daughter*. When, a week or so later, I met the writer again and told him I'd read *The Captain's Daughter*, his face brightened and he asked, 'How does Pushkin describe St Petersburg in *The Captain's Daughter*?' I went through the story in my head; it was still fresh, but I had no answer for him. I couldn't recall any description of St Petersburg even though I knew the story's last scene was set there. I became even more puzzled that evening when I went back to the Pushkin to see how he described St Petersburg: he didn't. 'With Pushkin,' the writer said when we met again, 'he'll do one or two things. There'll be a coat hanging in the room. And the scene is there. No more needs to be said.'

'A coat hanging in the room. And the scene is there!' This was also what Manto could do. Like in *The Captain's Daughter*, in 'Ten Rupees' Bombay is hardly described. There's a single reference to bazaars clogging with traffic from cars, buses, trams and pedestrians as Sarita and the boys are leaving town, but that is all. Bombay is that factory wall with the stench of urine drifting down its entire stretch. And this quality of detail, seeming to contain an entire milieu in a few lines, runs right through Manto. In 'Khaled Mian', the stillness of the night as Mumtaz waits for news of his dying child: 'It was ten at night. The maidan was dark and silent. Sometimes the horn of a car would graze the silence as it went past. Up ahead, over a high wall, the illuminated hospital clock could be seen.' In 'Ram Khilavan', the austerity of the narrator's room: 'It was a tiny room, destitute of even an electric light. There was one table, one chair and one sack-covered cot with a thousand bedbugs.' In 'My Name is Radha', a restaurant where all the movie people came: 'I'd spend whole days at Gulab's Hotel, drinking tea. Everyone who came in was either partially or entirely drenched. The flies too, seeking shelter from the rain, collected within. It was squalid beyond words. A squeezed rag for making tea was draped on one chair; on another, lay a foul smelling knife, used for cutting onions, but now idle.' Though Manto's economy can be seen in each of these stories, nowhere is it more fully realised than in 'Ram Khilavan'.

In under ten pages of short sentences, each sprung like a cricket bat, he conveys what feels like an entire lifetime in Bombay. The thread of the story is a relationship between the narrator and his dhobi. When the narrator is poor and living in a 'tiny room, destitute of even an electric light', the dhobi, illiterate and warmhearted, overlooks his unpaid bills. The narrator's fortunes improve, he gets married, moves to a bigger place, the dhobi continues to come. One day the dhobi falls sick with alcohol poisoning and the narrator's wife takes him in a car to the doctor, and so, saves his life. The dhobi never forgets this kindness. Then Partition happens, the city is inflamed with Hindu–Muslim riots and the narrator decides to leave for Pakistan. On his last evening in Bombay, he goes to the dhobi to pick up his clothes. The curfew hour is approaching and he finds himself surrounded by a murderous mob of drunken dhobis, of whom one is his. The dhobi, in a drunken haze, is about to attack the narrator when he recognises him. The next day, the narrator's last in Bombay, the dhobi brings the clothes as usual. He is overwhelmed with regret, but is never really able to express himself. A few hours later, the narrator leaves Bombay, never to return. The sense of loss and futility, told through this story of the little people one knew and has now to leave behind, is devastating. So much else is contained in the story's compass: the nature of Partition violence; the kind of person who fell prey to it; how relationships in a city can change through such violence. The writer seems to be writing from deep within his material so that none of this is added externally, but is part of the fiction's logic. The economy is not forced or done simply for the sake of economy; it feels necessary, an aspect of the story's urgency.

Given the extent to which Manto inhabits his material, there is something miraculous, like with Maupassant, whom Manto read and admired, that his range should have been so vast. He wrote about prostitution, religious superstition, adolescent anxiety, sex, the Partition of India and Bombay cinema in the thirties and forties. They were the great themes of his time and though the stories are not forgiving, nor do they falsify the hard realities of India, there is something euphoric in the writing; it is easy to sense the writer's joy in the newness and variety of life.

Manto investigated these themes, using sometimes a third person narrator, and sometimes, as in 'Ram Khilavan', a narrator called Manto. Manto, the narrator, should not be confused with Manto, the man or the writer. He is like the narrators used by Proust and VS Naipaul, and though travelling under the writer's name, he is, if anything, a more forceful creation of the imagination. Nor are the stories any less a work of fiction than if an omniscient, third person narrator had been used. This kind of narrator is not a gimmick; he serves a distinct purpose. In an immigrant city like Bombay, where no cultural knowledge can be assumed, where the landscape is often foreign and various, Manto, the fictional presence, declares his outsider's perspective and becomes a kind of guide to the new terrain. He marks out the world; the reader can put himself in his hands; his discoveries become part of the narrative. His gaze, like in 'Ten Rupees', is always oblique and a little perverse. The situation of women in society might be dealt with through the anger of an affronted prostitute, an adolescent's sexual discovery through a satin blouse.

It is hard not to come to feel a great affection for this narrator. He is mischievous, compassionate, funny, a listener, a drinker, sceptical and without prejudice. His Bombay is a city of motor cars and bicycles, of chawls and mansions, of hookers and heiresses, of Sikhs and Parsis, of depressives and lunatics, and he asserts his nativity by moving freely between its varied lives, making it seem like no less his right than sitting on a bench at Apollo Bandar, watching boats and people go by. At one point in her essay, 'My Friend, My Enemy', Manto's great friend, Ismat Chughtai, questions a description Manto gives to her of a friend of his.

> That he could be a rascal and at the same time an extremely honest and honourable man, how could that be? I didn't even try to understand. This was Manto's territory. From the jilted squalor and refuse of life, he picks out pearls. He enjoys digging in the refuse because he doesn't trust the luminaries of the world; he doesn't trust their brilliance or their judgement. He catches the thieves that lie in the hearts of their pure and respectable wives. And he compares them to the purity in the heart of a whore in a brothel.

As much as one would like to separate Manto, the writer, from Manto, the man, it is not always easy to do so. There is the added confusion of how much Manto's main narrator seems to resemble both writer and man. All of this makes it harder to bear that ugly truth about Manto, the man: that for all his love of Indian multiplicity, he went to Pakistan. He even tried convincing Chughtai to go. 'The future looks beautiful in Pakistan,' he said to her, 'We'll be able to get the houses of people who've fled from there. It'll be just us there. We'll progress very quickly.' When I read this, I had trouble holding the two Mantos in my mind. It seemed impossible that the creator of Manto, the narrator and fictional presence, so immersed in the variety of India, seeming so much to rejoice in it, should also be the author of that remark, with its sly wish for homogeneity, for the place where 'It'll be just us.' Chughtai, for other reasons, was also disgusted. The two had an intensely close friendship. He spoke movingly to her about the son he'd lost, giving details about bathing him, and how he would pick up things from the floor and put them in his mouth, details which seem to have fed directly into 'Khaled Mian'. Manto and Chughtai argued and fought and laughed about everything from love and relationships to language and literature, but never seriously, except over Pakistan. 'I'd had so many fights and arguments with him,' she wrote, 'but never over a serious matter of principle. In that moment, I realised what a coward Manto was. He was ready to save his life at any cost. To make his future, he was ready to get his hands on the life earnings of people who were fleeing. And I began to feel a hatred for him.'

Manto did not just regret his decision to go to Pakistan; it destroyed him. In his stunning essay on the 1949 'Cold Flesh' trial (in which, it must be said, my grandfather, though he said little to damn him, appeared on the side of the prosecution) in Lahore, he pointedly answers Chughtai's charge of taking part in the property grab and denies ever having done so. He also seems very early to anticipate the larger cultural questions the Partition would bring up for both Pakistan and India. He wrote of his arrival in Lahore:

Try as I did, I wasn't able to separate Pakistan from India and India from Pakistan. Again and again, troubling questions rang in my mind: Will Pakistan's literature be separate from that of India's? If so, how? Who owns all that was written in undivided India? Will that be partitioned too? Are India's and Pakistan's core problems not the same? Will Urdu be totally wiped out in India? What shape will it take here in Pakistan? Will our state be a religious one? We'll defend the state at all cost, but does that mean we won't have permission to criticise its government? As an independent country, will our condition be different from what it was under the British?

In Pakistan, Manto was tried twice for obscenity. He and Chughtai had faced obscenity trials before Independence as well, but there is a marked difference in the tone of his descriptions of the pre-Partition trials versus those in Pakistan. There is a lightness about the earlier trials: he travels up to Lahore with Chughtai; they buy slippers along the way; and at the 1941 trial of 'Smoke', he seems to be having a positively good time, lecturing the court on Maupassant. But in Pakistan, the trials were longer, more exacting, and the outcome, more disturbing; there were arrests, searches and the risk of jail time with hard labour. In January 1952, in between trials, Manto wrote,

My mind was in a strange state. I couldn't understand what I should do. Whether I should stop writing or carry on totally regardless of this scrutiny. Truth be told, it had left such a bad taste that I almost wished some place would be allotted to me where I could sit in one corner, away for some years from pens and ink wells; should thoughts arise in my mind, I would hang them at the gallows; and should an allotment not be possible, I could begin work as a black marketeer or start distilling illicit alcohol…

It was the latter that finally claimed Manto. His last years were beset with financial troubles; he drank heavily; he wrote to Chughtai on more than one occasion, pleading with her to find a way for him to come back to India. She was surprised to learn that far from large protests and signed declarations on his behalf, many in Pakistan felt he deserved to be punished. He died on January 18, 1955 in Lahore at the age of forty two.

In death, Manto paid a greater price for his migration than he had when he was alive. He was forgotten in the country he wrote most about. He became part of a number of artists, musicians and writers whom India disowned—sometimes by singling them out, sometimes as part of a larger disowning of Urdu—for their migration. It might appear strange to someone reading this collection why I, with my mixed Indian and Pakistani heritage, have included so few of Manto's famous Partition stories in this collection. The reason is that I found, with their simple symmetries, drenched in that bittersweet irony of how one people could have ended up as two nations, they were the only stories of Manto's two hundred and fifty that today, feel dated. But it is also for this reason, because so little has ended up as symmetrical in the fortunes of India and Pakistan, that India must now reclaim men like Manto. In Pakistan, Manto's world, crowded with

Hindus, Sikhs and Muslims, would feel very foreign. It is only in India, still plural, not symmetrically Hindu, that it continues to have relevance. His eye could only have been an Indian eye, sensitive to surprising detail, compulsively aware of Indian plurality, sympathetic to people trapped in their circumstances, here pointing to a particular Hindu festival, there imitating Bombay street dialect.

Writers rarely set out to be national writers. They need small, intimate worlds, full of details; the macro scale of countries, especially those as wide and various as India, cannot be their direct material. Cities, neighbourhoods, sometimes a single street, provide the gritty detail in which a larger architecture can become visible. For Manto, this city, as Dublin was for Joyce and Chicago for Bellow, was Bombay. He was not an Indian or Pakistani writer as much as he was a Bombay writer, and more than India, the city of Bombay must reclaim Manto.

Khalid Hasan, Manto's Pakistani translator, has done what he can to make Manto available in English, and though exhaustive, his translations not only lack the simplicity, speed and vitality of Manto's prose, they are guilty of the greatest crime any translator can commit, the crime of trying to improve upon the writer. This well meaning journalist paraphrases Manto; he deletes entire paragraphs in 'For Freedom'; and rearranges chunks of text in 'Blouse', even deciding to change the colour of the blouse from purple or violet to 'azure'. The result is that his translations are not really close translations at all; they are synopses.

Having said this, the challenges of translating Manto are considerable. What is rich, fluent prose in Urdu can appear florid in English; Manto leaves loose ends, his sentences can be mangled. He also becomes a victim of his form, namely the short story's dependence on trick and surprise endings. David Coward, in his introduction to Maupassant's stories, writes,

> For the short story, while admitted to be extremely difficult to manage successfully, has long been regarded as somehow second rate, not least because it is generally felt to suffer from Cleverness. Perhaps it requires too much control, so that the reader feels manipulated, and because many short stories depend so much on irony or sudden reversals, they may seem overcontrived—like a joke which, once told, loses its tension.

For the reader of the novel especially, this kind of ending can be hard to stomach. In stories like 'My Name is Radha', and even 'Licence', one is almost left wishing for an unfinished ending rather than the one of high drama. And yet, I feel in the end, it is better for the translator to lay himself at the feet of his subject than try, at this late stage, to tidy him up, especially when dealing with as natural and gifted a writer as Manto. Translations are often criticised for being too literal, but in the case of Manto's translators, I feel they haven't been literal enough, that they have tried to rewrite the stories. This translation aims at being very literal, relishing especially, the feeling of the other language breaking through. The stories I have selected are only a few, but they show Manto's range both in style and subject.

The translations became a way for me, with my mixed

heritage, to limit the effects of the intellectual partition Manto feared. The linking of language to religion, followed by the partition along religious lines, has left the subcontinent's intellectual past fenced up and pitted with no go zones; it has constantly to be sorted through, constantly to be excavated and reclaimed. The translations were part of a larger feeling in me that I would rather end up with Sanskrit and Urdu than neither. It was English, both for its impartiality and the opportunity its literary life offers, that made this possible. And for the same reasons, translations of Manto into English become important. It is a strange truth about Indian intellectual life that the road to rediscovering a writer like Manto in the original is bound to run first through English.

But for those without English, men like Zafar Moradabadi, who became an Urdu poet when it was still possible to do so, the currents of intellectual life have washed them up on less secure shores.

Zafar lives in the Sui Valan section of the old city of Delhi. I went to his house for the first time one smoky December night, on Eid. He picked me up outside Delite cinema, admonishing me for bringing him flowers and sweets. As we entered the old city, some men from the abattoir were unloading a truckload of meat. The rickshaw splashed through a pale, brownish-red puddle; the smell and the frenzy of flies gave it away as blood. Narrow streets, crowded that night with bright kerosene lights and people in their new clothes, led to Zafar's house. We arrived in front of a darkened entrance. Near an open drain, a bitch tended to her family of fluffy grey puppies. A flight of steep stone stairs, chipped at the edges, led up to a pale green door and a landing, lit by a single light.

Zafar had warned me many times on the way how small his house was. 'But the hearts of the people in it are big,' he added. I had imagined his house would be a small flat, with a kitchen, a bathroom, two rooms perhaps, at least room enough to stand up, to walk around. But Zafar's house was a single room, no bigger than a carpet, covered with sheets of chequered cloth. Its pistachio green walls were high and there were shelves all around, stacked to the ceiling with hard suitcases and trunks so that it felt almost like being in a godown. Everything was neatly in its place: a sewing machine with a pink satin cover, necessary where clothes are repaired often; a little shelf with holy Zam Zam water, oils and a pair of scissors; green-covered copies of Zafar's new book. There was no kitchen, just a ledge with pulses and grains stacked high on one side. Its stone surface was used for washing, the water disappearing through an opening in the floor. The bathroom was a single metal sheet, leading to a drain. Everything was hanging—towels, toothbrushes, clothes, including a green bra, all heaped over a nylon rope. The air was fetid and filled the little room.

Zafar's family of five couldn't physically fit in the room and he slept on the floor of a magazine office in another part of the old city, near Ghalib's old house. He had once saved enough money to buy a better place. But in 1997, the year when the accounts had become computerised, his wife had fallen from the stairs and all his savings were spent on her treatment. She was there now, dressed in a black kameez with red flowers on it. She was a fat woman, with curly hair and pale skin. She was smiling, and though her face was made up, something in her eyes suggested damage, almost as if they were unused to emotions other than distress.

That night, as we ate a small feast on an oil cloth in the little room, a number of strong feelings occurred to me at once. There was the very romantic idea of the old city, even in total collapse, as still sheltering poets; there was the miracle of Zafar and his family retaining their refinement despite the squalor around them; there was also a feeling of dread for India, for any country that would let its men of learning live in conditions like these. When I thought harder about it, I was struck by how genteel and unlikely a calamity this was. Urdu had not died, but its literary culture in India had, and it had left its casualties, of which Zafar was one. His fate had been tied up with the fate of the language. I found it suddenly painful to think that the man who had helped me to understand and translate had himself ended up a prisoner of language. He had once said to me, 'There is knowledge. Everything else comes and goes.' But only now, seeing him in the poverty and decay that threatened always to diminish him, I understood how he must have clung to that exalted idea; and how at times, it must have been so difficult to defend. He had also reminded me, in relation to Urdu, that I had a tradition to uphold. The words then were just part of a lively argument; I hadn't known about the life spent in service of that tradition, even as the infrastructure of literature collapsed around him. Zafar had also described himself as an intellectual mercenary. But here, as I'd found so often with him, he was only half right. There was no denying that the life that had aged him and left him covered in sores, himself like a tattered page out of Manto, had been a fighting life. But what had been fought for was not fortune, but his gentle manners, his decency and the six hundred years of poetry ready on his blackened lips. And watching Zafar Moradabadi sit back against the wall, smoking a Win cigarette, it was not so much the mercenary that came to mind as the martyr.

Aatish Taseer, New Delhi, 2008

Ten Rupees

She was playing with the little girls at the far end of the alley. Inside the chawl, her mother hunted for her everywhere. Kishori sat waiting in their room; someone had been told to bring him tea. Sarita's mother now began searching for her on all three floors of the chawl. Who knew which hole Sarita had gone and died in? She even went into the bathrooms, yelling, 'Sarita... Sarita!' But Sarita, as her mother was beginning to realise, was not in the chawl. She was outside on the corner of the alley, near a heap of garbage, playing with the little girls, utterly carefree.

Her mother was in a panic. Kishori sat waiting in the room; the men he'd brought—as promised, two rich men, with a motor car—waited in the main market; but where had her daughter vanished to? She couldn't even use the excuse of dysentery anymore; she was well now. And rich men with motor cars didn't come every day. It was Kishori's benevolence that once or twice a month, he managed to bring clients with motor cars. Normally he was nervous of neighbourhoods like this, with their compound stench of paan and stale bidis. How could he bring rich men here? But because he was smart, Kishori never brought the men to the chawl. Instead, he brought Sarita, bathed and clothed, to them, explaining that 'these are uncertain times; the place is crawling with police spies; they've taken away nearly a hundred working girls; there's even a case against me in the courts; one has to tread very carefully.'

Sarita's mother had by now become very angry. When she came down, Ramdi was sitting at the bottom of the stairs, cutting leaves for the bidis as usual. 'Have you seen Sarita anywhere?' Sarita's mother demanded, 'God knows which hole she's gone and died in. And today of all days! Wait till I find her! I'll give her a thrashing she'll remember in every joint of her body. She's a full grown woman, you know, and all she ever does is waste the day fooling around with kids.'

Ramdi said nothing and continued to cut the bidi leaves. But Sarita's mother wasn't really speaking to her; she was just ranting as usual as she walked past. Every few days, she would go off in search of Sarita, and repeat the same words to Ramdi.

Sarita's mother would also tell the chawl's women that she wanted Sarita to marry a clerk some day. This was why she had always impressed upon Sarita the importance of education. The municipality had opened a school nearby and Sarita's mother wondered if she should admit her daughter there. 'Sister, you know, her father had such a desire that his daughter should be educated!' At this point she would sigh, and repeat the story of her dead husband, which every woman in the chawl knew by heart. If you were to say to Ramdi, 'Alright, when Sarita's father worked in the railways and the big sahib insulted him, what happened?' she would immediately reply, 'Sarita's father foamed at the mouth and said to the sahib, "I'm not your servant; I'm the government's servant. You have no right to throw your weight round here. And careful—you insult me again and I'll rip your jaws out and shove them down your throat." Then, what?

What was bound to happen happened! The sahib was livid and insulted Sarita's father again. Sarita's father came forward and delivered such a powerful blow to the sahib's neck that his hat flew off his head and landed ten paces away and he saw stars in the daytime! But the sahib was not a small man either. He retaliated by kicking Sarita's father on the back with his army boot, and with such force that his spleen burst, and there and then, by the railway lines, he fell to the floor and breathed his last. The government ran a court case against the sahib and extracted a full five hundred rupees in compensation from him for Sarita's mother. But her luck was bad. She developed a taste for the lottery, and within five months, she had squandered the money.'

This story was always ready on Sarita's mother's lips, but nobody was sure whether or not it was true. In any case, it didn't evoke any compassion for her in the chawl, perhaps because everyone there was also deserving of compassion. And no one was anyone's friend. The men, by and large, slept during the day and were awake at night as many worked the night shift at the nearby mill. They lived together, but they showed no interest in each other's lives.

In the chawl, virtually everyone knew that Sarita's mother had sent her young daughter into prostitution. But since these were people who treated each other neither well nor badly, they felt no need to expose her when she'd say, 'My daughter knows nothing of this world.'

One morning, when Tukaram made an advance on Sarita, her mother began to screech and yell, 'For God's sake, why doesn't anyone control this wretched baldy?

3

May the lord make him blind in both the eyes with which he ogles my virgin daughter! I swear, one day, there'll be such a brawl that I'll take this darling of yours and beat his head to a pulp with the heel of my shoe. Outside, he can do whatever he wants, but in here he'd better learn to behave like a decent human being, do you hear?'

Hearing this, Tukaram's cross-eyed wife appeared, knotting her dhoti as she approached. 'You wretched witch, don't you dare let one more word escape your lips! This virginal daughter of yours even makes eyes at the boys who hang around the hotel... Do you think we're all blind? You think we don't know of the clerks who come to your house? This daughter of yours, Sarita, why does she get all made up and go out? You really have some nerve, coming in here with airs of respectability. Go get lost, somewhere far away, go on!'

There were many well-known stories about Tukaram's cross-eyed wife. Everyone knew that when the kerosene oil dealer would come with his kerosene, she would take him into her quarter and lock the door. Sarita's mother loved to draw attention to this. In a voice brimming with hatred, she would repeat, 'And your lover, the kerosene oil dealer... Two hours at a time, you keep him locked up in your quarter, what are you doing? Sniffing his kerosene oil?'

The spats between Tukaram's wife and Sarita's mother never lasted long because one night Sarita's mother had caught her neighbour exchanging sweet nothings with someone in pitch darkness. And the very next night, Tukaram's wife had seen Sarita with a 'gentleman man' in a motor car. As a result, the two women had made a pact

4

between themselves, which is why Sarita's mother now said to Tukaram's wife, 'Have you seen Sarita anywhere?'

Tukaram wife's turned her squinting eye in the direction of the street corner, 'There, near the dump. She's playing with the manager's girls.' Then in a lower voice, she added, 'Kishori's just gone upstairs. Did you see him?'

Sarita's mother looked around her and in a still lower voice said, 'He's sitting inside... But Sarita's never to be found at such times. She doesn't think, she understands nothing, all she does is spend the day running around.' With this, Sarita's mother walked towards the dump. Sarita jumped up when she saw her mother approaching the cemented urinal, the laughter leaving her eyes... Her mother grabbed her arm roughly and said, 'Come on, come into the house, come in and die... Do you have nothing better to do than play these rowdy games?' On the way in, in a softer voice, she said, 'Kishori's here. He's been waiting a long time. He's brought men with motor cars. Go on, run upstairs and get dressed. And wear that blue georgette sari of yours. Oh and listen, your hair's a terrible mess, get dressed quickly and I'll come up and comb it.'

Sarita was very happy to hear that rich men with motor cars had come for her, granted she was more interested in the motor cars than in the rich men who drove them. She loved riding in motor cars. When the car would roar down the open streets and the wind would slap her face, then everything would become a whirlwind and she would feel like a tornado tearing down empty streets.

Sarita was no older than fifteen, but with the interests of a girl of thirteen. She didn't like spending time with grown women at all. Her entire day was taken up, playing silly games with the younger girls. They liked especially to draw chalk lines on the street's black tar surface, and remained so absorbed in this game that one might almost believe that the street's traffic depended on them drawing their crooked little lines. Sometimes Sarita would bring out old pieces of sackcloth from her room. And for hours she and her young friends, would remain immersed in the singularly monotonous business of dusting them and laying them out on the footpath to sit on.

Sarita was not beautiful. Her skin was a dusky wheat colour, its texture smooth and glistening in Bombay's humid climate. Her thin lips, like sapodilla skins, also blackish, were always quivering faintly and a few tiny beads of sweat trembled on her upper lip. She looked robust despite living in squalor; her body was short, pleasing and well-proportioned. She gave the impression that the sheer vitality of her youth had subdued all contrary forces. Men on the streets gazed at her calves whenever her dirty skirt flew up in the wind. Youth had bestowed on them the shine of polished teak. These calves, entirely unacquainted with hair, had small marks on them that recalled orange skins with tiny, juice-filled pores, ready to erupt like fountains at the slightest pressure.

Her arms were also pleasing. The attractive roundness of her shoulders made itself apparent through the baggy, badly stitched blouse she wore. Her hair was thick and long, with the smell of coconut oil rising from it. Her plait, thick like a whip, would thump against her back. But the length of her hair made her unhappy as it got in the way of the games she played; she had invented various ways of keeping it under control.

Sarita was free of all worry and anxiety. She had enough to eat twice a day. Her mother handled all their household affairs. Every morning Sarita filled buckets of water and took them inside; every evening she filled the lamp with one paisa's worth of oil. Her hand reached habitually every evening for the cup with the money, and taking the lamp, she'd make her way downstairs.

Sarita had come to think of her visits to hotels and dimly lit places with rich men, which Kishori organised four or five times a month, as jaunts. She never gave any thought to the other aspects of these jaunts. She might even have believed that men like Kishori came to all the other girls' houses too and that they also went on outings with rich men. And what happened on Worli's cold benches and Juhu's wet beaches, perhaps happened to all the other girls as well. On one occasion she even said to her mother: 'Ma, Shanta's quite old now. Why not send her along with me too? The rich men who just came took me to eat eggs and Shanta loves eggs.' Sarita's mother parried the question. 'Yes, yes, some day I'll send her along with you. Let her mother return from Pune, no?' Sarita relayed the good news to Shanta the next day, when she saw her coming out of the bathroom. 'When your mother returns from Pune, everything will be alright. You're going to come with me to Worli too!' Sarita began to recount the night's activities as if she was reliving a beautiful dream. Shanta, two years younger than Sarita, felt little bells ring through her body as she listened to Sarita. Even when she'd heard all Sarita had to say, she

7

was unsatisfied. She grabbed her by the arm and said, 'Come on, let's go downstairs where we can talk.' There, near the urinal where Girdhari the merchant had laid out dirty coconut husks to dry on gunny sacks, the two girls spoke till late about subjects that made them tingle with excitement.

Now, as she changed hurriedly into her blue georgette sari behind a makeshift curtain, she was aware of the cloth tickling her skin, and her thoughts, like the fluttering of a bird's wings, returned to riding in the motor car. What would the rich men be like this time; where would they take her? These, and other such questions, didn't enter her mind. She worried instead that the motor would run only for a few short minutes before their arrival at the door of some hotel. She didn't like to be confined to the four walls of hotel rooms, with their two metal beds, which were not really meant for her to fall asleep on.

She put on the georgette sari, and smoothing its creases, came and stood for a moment in front of Kishori. 'Take a look, Kishori, it's alright from the back, no?' Without waiting for a reply, she moved towards the broken wooden suitcase in which the Japanese powder and rouge were kept. She took a dusty mirror, wedged it between the window rods, and bending down, put a mixture of rouge and powder on her cheeks. When she was completely ready, she smiled and looked at Kishori, her eyes seeking appreciation.

She resembled one of those painted clay figures that appear during Diwali as the showpiece in a toy shop, with her bright blue sari, lipstick carelessly smudged on her lips, onion pink powder on her dark cheeks.

In the meantime, her mother arrived. She did Sarita's hair quickly and said, 'Listen, darling, speak nicely to the men and do whatever they ask. They are important; they've come in a motor car.' Then addressing Kishori, she said, 'Now, hurry up, take her to them. Poor fellows, I don't know how long they've been left waiting.'

In the main market, a yellow car was parked outside a long factory wall, near a small board that read, 'It is forbidden to urinate here'. Inside, the three young Hyderabadi men waiting for Kishori held their handkerchiefs to their noses. They would have liked to park the car ahead somewhere, but the factory wall was long and the stench of urine drifted down its entire stretch. When the young man who sat at the wheel caught sight of Kishori at the street corner, he said to his two other friends, 'Well, brothers, he's come. It's Kishori and... and... ' He fixed his gaze on the street corner. 'And... and... well, she's just a little girl! You take a look... that one, man... the one in the blue sari.'

When Kishori and Sarita approached, the two young men sitting in the back removed their hats and made room for her in the middle. Kishori reached forward, opened the door and swiftly installed Sarita in the back. Closing the door, he said to the young man at the wheel, 'Forgive me, we were delayed; she was at one of her friends' places. Well, so?'

The young man turned around and looked at Sarita, then said to Kishori: 'Alright, but listen... ' He slid across the seat and appeared at the other window. Whispering in Kishori's ear, he said, 'She's not going to kick up a fuss, is she?'

Kishori placed his hand over his chest in reply. 'Sir! You must have faith in me.' Hearing this, the young man took two rupees out of his pocket and handed them to Kishori. 'Go, have fun!'

Kishori waved them off and Kafayat started the engine.

It was five in the evening. Bombay's bazaars were clogging with traffic from cars, buses, trams and pedestrians. Sarita was lost between the two young men. She would keep her thighs clamped tightly together, place her hands over them and start to say something, then mid-sentence, fall into silence. What she would have liked to say to the young man driving was, 'For God's sake, let it rip. I'm suffocating in here.'

For a long time, no one said anything. The young man at the wheel continued to drive and the two young Hyderabadis in the back, under their long, dark coats, suppressed their nervousness at being so close to a young girl for the first time, a young girl whom, for at least a while, they could call their own and touch without fear or danger.

The young man at the wheel had been living in Bombay for the past two years and had seen many girls like Sarita, both in daylight and at night. His yellow car had hosted girls of various shade and quality and so he felt no great nervousness now. Of his two friends who had come from Hyderabad, one, who went by the name of Shahab, wanted a full tour of Bombay. And it was with this in mind that Kafayat—the young owner of the car—out of friendship, asked Kishori to organise Sarita. To his other friend, Anwar, Kafayat said, 'Listen, man, if there ends up being one for you too, what harm is there?' But, Anwar, less assertive, never overcame his shyness enough to say, 'Yes, get one for me too.'

Kafayat had never seen Sarita before—it had been a while since Kishori had brought a new girl. Despite this, Kafayat showed no interest in her, perhaps because a man can only do one thing at a time and he couldn't drive as well as turn his attention to her. Once they'd left the city and the car came on to a country road, Sarita jumped up. The car's sudden speed and the gusts of cold air that came in lifted the restraints she had put on herself until now. Bursts of electricity ran though her entire body. Her legs throbbed, her arms seemed to dance, her fingers trembled and she watched the trees race past her on both sides.

Anwar and Shahab were now at ease. Shahab, who felt he had first rights to Sarita, gently moved his arm forward, wanting to place it around her back. The movement tickled her; she jumped up and landed on Anwar with a thump. Her laughter flowed out of the windows of the yellow car and carried into the distance. When Shahab tried again to place his hand on her back, she bent double with laughter. Anwar, hidden in one corner of the car, sat in silence, his mouth dry.

Shahab's mind filled with bright colours. He said to Kafayat, 'My God, man, she's a little minx.' With this, he violently pinched Sarita's thigh. In reply, and because he was closest to her, Sarita gently twisted Anwar's ear. The car erupted in laughter.

Kafayat kept turning around even though everything was visible to him in his rearview mirror. He added to the growing commotion in the back by speeding up the car.

11

Sarita wished she could climb out and ride on the bonnet of the car where the flying iron fairy was. She moved forward. Shahab reached for her and to steady herself, she wrapped her arms around Kafayat's neck. Without meaning to, he kissed them. A shiver went through her entire body and she leapt into the front seat of the car and began to play with Kafayat's tie. 'What is your name,' she asked Kafayat.

'My name!' he said. 'My name is Kafayat.' With this, he put a ten rupee note in her hand. She paid no further attention to his name, but squeezed the note into her blouse, brimming with childish happiness. 'You're a very nice man. And this tie of yours is also very nice.'

In that instant, Sarita saw goodness in everything and wished that all that was bad would also turn to good... and... and... then it would happen... the motor would continue to race and everything around her would become part of the whirlwind.

She suddenly felt the urge to sing. So she stopped playing with Kafayat's tie and began: 'You taught me how to love, and stirred a sleeping heart.'

For some time, the film song continued and then Sarita turned to Anwar who was sitting in silence. 'Why are you so quiet, say something, sing something!' With this, she jumped into the back seat again and began running her fingers through Shahab's hair. 'Come on, both of you, sing. You remember that song that Devika Rani used to sing? "I'm a sparrow in the heart's jungle, singing my little song..." Devika Rani is so good, isn't she?'

Then she put both her hands under her thighs, and fluttering her eyelids, said, 'Ashok Kumar and Devika Rani stood close to each other. Devika Rani would say, "I'm a sparrow in the forest, singing my little song." And Ashok Kumar would say, "Sing it then." '

Sarita began the song. 'I'm a sparrow in the forest, singing my little song.'

Shahab in a loud, coarse voice answered, 'I'll become a forest bird and sing from forest to forest.'

And all of a sudden, a duet began. Kafayat provided accompaniment on the car horn. Sarita began to clap. Her thin soprano, Shahab's coarse singing, the horn's honking, the blasts of wind and the roar of the engine, came together to form an orchestra.

Sarita was happy; Shahab was happy; Kafayat was happy, and seeing them all happy, Anwar was forced to be happy. He regretted his earlier restraint. His arms began to move. His sleeping heart had stirred and he was ready now to be a part of Sarita, Shahab and Kafayat's boisterous happiness.

As they sang, Sarita removed Anwar's hat from his head and put it on her own. She leapt into the front seat again and gazed at herself in the small mirror to see how it looked. Had he really been wearing his hat all this time? Anwar thought.

Sarita slapped Kafayat's fat thigh and said, 'If I wear your trousers and your shirt and put on a tie like this one, will I become a pukka gentleman too?'

Hearing this, Shahab couldn't decide what he should do. He yanked Anwar's arm: 'You've been a complete idiot.' And for a moment, Anwar believed he was right.

Kafayat asked Sarita, 'What is your name?'

'My name!' Sarita replied, slipping the hat's strap under her chin. 'My name is Sarita.'

'Sarita,' Shahab said from the back seat, 'you're not a woman; you're a livewire.'

Anwar wanted to say something too but Sarita began to sing in a high voice.

'In love town, I'll build my house… forgoing all the worrrrrld.'

And bits of that world flew around them. Sarita's hair, no longer bound by her plait, broke free and scattered like dark smoke dispersed by wind; she was happy.

Shahab was happy; Kafayat was happy and now Anwar, too, was ready to be happy. The song ended; for a few moments everyone felt that it had just been raining hard and had now abruptly stopped.

'Any more songs?' Kafayat asked Sarita.

'Yes, yes,' Shahab said from the back, 'let's have one more. One that even these film people won't forget!'

Sarita began again. 'Spring came to my house. And I, I hit the road, a little drunkenly.'

The car also wove drunkenly. Then the road straightened and the seashore came in sight. The sun was setting and the sea wind brought a chill in the air.

The car stopped. Sarita opened the door, jumped out and began to run along the shore. Kafayat and Shahab ran behind her. In the open air, on the edge of the vast ocean, with the great palms rising up from the wet sand, Sarita didn't know what it was that she wanted. She wished she could melt into the sky; spread through the ocean; fly so high that she could see the palm canopies

14

from above; for all the wetness of the shore to seep from the sand into her feet and then... and then for that same racing engine, that same speed, those blasts of wind, the car honking—she was very happy.

The three young Hyderabadi men sat down on the wet sand and opened their beers. Sarita snatched the bottle from Kafayat's hand. 'Wait, I'll pour it.'

She poured it so that the glass filled with foam. The spectacle of it excited her. She put her finger into the brownish foam, then into her mouth. She made a face when she tasted its bitterness. Kafayat and Shahab laughed uncontrollably. Still laughing, Kafayat looked over at Anwar and saw that he was laughing too.

They went through six bottles of beer; some entered their stomachs; some turned to foam and was absorbed by the sand. Sarita continued to sing. Anwar looked in her direction and thought for a moment that she was made of beer. In the sea's moist air, her dark cheeks had become wet. She felt a deep contentment. Anwar now, was happy too. He wanted the sea to turn to beer; to go diving in it; and for Sarita to join him.

Sarita took two empty bottles and banged them together. They made a clatter and she laughed. Kafayat, Anwar and Shahab laughed too.

Still laughing, Sarita said to Kafayat, 'Come on, let's drive the car now.'

Everyone rose. Empty beer bottles lay strewn on the wet sand. The party ran to the car. Once again, the wind began to blast, the horn honked, and Sarita's hair scattered like dark smoke. The singing resumed.

The car plowed through the wind. Sarita continued

to sing. She sat in the back between Anwar and Shahab. Anwar's head dropped from side to side. Sarita mischievously began to comb Shahab's hair with her fingers and he fell asleep. When she turned back to Anwar, she saw that he was also fast asleep. She lifted herself from in between them and lowered herself into the front seat.

In a whisper, she said, 'I've just put both your friends to bed. Now, I'll put you to bed too.'

Kafayat smiled. 'Who'll drive the car then?'

Sarita, smiling as well, replied, 'It'll keep running.'

For a long time, they spoke among themselves. The bazaar reappeared. When they drove past the wall with the small board that read, 'It is forbidden to urinate here', Sarita said, 'Just here is fine.'

The car stopped. Sarita jumped out before Kafayat was able to do or say anything. She waved and walked away. Kafayat sat with one hand on the wheel, perhaps thinking back on the day's events.

Then Sarita stopped, turned around, walked back, and from her blouse, removed a ten rupee note and placed it next to him.

Kafayat stared at it in amazement. 'Sarita, what's this?'

'This… why should I take this money?' she replied and ran off, leaving Kafayat still staring at the limp note.

He turned around eventually. Anwar and Shahab, like the note itself, lay slumped in the back seat, asleep.

Blouse

Momin had been feeling unsettled for the past few days. His body was as raw as a boil. He felt a mysterious pain, while working, while talking, even while thinking. But had he tried to describe it, he would have been unable to.

He would sometimes start while sitting. Hazy thoughts that usually rose and vanished soundlessly like bubbles in his mind, now burst, with great fury. Ants with barbed feet seemed to crawl over the pathways of his tender mind. A tightness had arisen in his body, and it caused him terrible discomfort. When it became too much, he'd wish he was in a giant cauldron, ready to be ground down.

He felt a deep satisfaction at hearing masalas being crushed in the kitchen: the noise of metal clashing with metal ringing out like a threat into the recesses of the roof, where he stood barefoot. The vibrations would run up his bare feet, to his taut calves and thighs, before reaching his heart, which would flutter like the flame of a clay lamp in a fast wind.

Momin was fifteen, perhaps sixteen; he didn't know his exact age. He was a strong, healthy boy whose pubescence galloped towards adulthood and it was the effects of this gallop—of which Momin was wholly ignorant—that throbbed in every drop of his blood. He tried to comprehend its meaning, but he couldn't.

Changes in his body were also becoming apparent. His neck, once thin, was thickening; his Adam's apple was becoming more prominent; the muscles in his arms had grown tighter; his chest had hardened, and it had swollen in places as if someone had squeezed marbles into it. Touching these lumps caused Momin great discomfort. His hand accidentally grazing them, or even his thick shirt brushing against them while he worked, would make him jump up with pain.

In the bathroom, or alone in the kitchen, he would undo the buttons of his shirt and carefully examine these lumps, massaging them lightly. Stabs of pain would shoot through him as if his body, like a tree heavy with fruit, had been shaken. And though it made him tremble, he would become absorbed in this painful pastime. Sometimes, if he pressed too hard, the lumps would puncture and release a sticky liquid. The sight of it made his face turn red to his ears. He felt that, without meaning to, he had committed a sin.

His knowledge, as far as sin and virtue went, was very limited. Anything that someone couldn't do in the presence of others struck him as a sin. And so whenever his face reddened to his ears, he hurriedly did up his shirt and swore to himself that he would never again engage in such inane pastimes. But despite these promises, two or three days later, he'd find himself once again absorbed in this activity.

Momin was turning the corner onto one of life's avenues, that was not as long as it was treacherous. He sometimes moved swiftly down it, sometimes slowly. The truth was that he didn't know how to traverse roads like these. Should they be negotiated as quickly as possible, or in a leisurely manner; should he perhaps take help along the way? He seemed to lose his footing on the slippery cobblestones of his approaching manhood; he had to fight to keep his balance. It perturbed him; it was the reason why, he would sometimes in the middle of his work, give a start, and grabbing a hook in the wall with both his hands, hang freely from it. Then he would have the urge for someone to hold his legs and pull him down until he became like a fine wire. But he couldn't understand the meaning of these thoughts, they seemed to arise from some unknown part of his brain.

Everyone in the household was happy with Momin. He was hardworking and did all his work on time so no one had any cause for complaint. He had only worked as a servant for three months, but in this short time, he'd impressed everyone in the house. He had begun at six rupees a month, but by the second month, his salary was raised by two rupees. He was happy in the house; he was shown respect here.

But now, in the past few days, he had become unsettled. The restlessness that took hold of him made him want to spend whole days wandering the bazaars, or to find some deserted spot where he could lie down.

He no longer had his heart in his work, but despite his listlessness, he hadn't become lazy, which was why no one in the house was aware of his inner turmoil. There was Razia who spent her entire day playing music, learning the newest film songs and reading magazines. She never paid any attention to Momin. Shakeela sometimes got Momin to do some work for her and even scolded him occasionally, but for the past few days, she, too, had been totally occupied, with copying the samples of a few blouses. They belonged to a friend of hers who kept up with the latest fashions. Shakeela had borrowed eight blouses from her and was copying them onto pieces of paper. And so, for the past few days, she hadn't paid much attention to Momin either.

The deputy saab's wife was not a severe woman. Other than Momin, there were two more servants in the house. There was an old lady who mostly worked in the kitchen; Momin occasionally lent her a hand. Deputy saab's wife might perhaps have noticed a change in Momin's alertness, but she hadn't mentioned it to him. She certainly knew nothing of the upheavals in his mind and body. She had no sons and so was unable to understand the changes he was experiencing. And besides, Momin was a servant. Who could pay that much attention to the lives of servants? They covered all life's stages on foot, from infancy to old age, and those around them never knew anything of it.

Though he was unaware of it, Momin was waiting for something to happen. For what? Just something: for the careful arrangement of plates on the table to start jumping up; for the water now coming to a boil to send the kettle's lid flying into the air; for the tap's lead pipe to crumple with the slightest pressure, and for a jet of water to shoot out; for his body to stretch, once and ever, so forcefully, that its every joint would come apart and hang loose; for something to reveal itself that he'd never experienced.

Momin was deeply unsettled.

And Razia was busy learning new film songs, and Shakeela copying blouse samples onto pieces of paper. When she'd finished doing this, she took the best of them and began making herself a blouse in violet satin.

Now even Razia was forced to leave her radio and filmi music and turn her attention towards this.

Shakeela always did everything with great care and composure. Her posture when she was sewing suggested contentment. She wasn't restless like her sister, Razia. Every stitch went on after careful consideration so that there was no room for error. Her measurements were always exact as she made paper cut-outs first, then used them to cut the cloth. This took more time, but the result was near perfect.

Shakeela was a large-bodied, healthy girl. She had thick, fleshy fingers, which tapered at the tips, and there were dimples at each joint. When she would work the sewing machine, they'd occasionally disappear with the movement of her hand.

Shakeela was just as calm at the machine. She would turn its wheel with two or three fingers, slowly and cleanly, her wrist gently arched. Her neck would bend forward slightly, and a lock of hair, unable to find a fixed place, would slip down. She would be so absorbed with her work that she wouldn't push it away.

Shakeela laid out the violet satin and was about to begin cutting the blouse in her size, when she realised she needed a tape measure. Their own tape was faded and falling to pieces; they had a metal one, but how could she measure her back and chest with that? She had many blouses of her own, but as she'd put on a little weight, she wanted to check all her measurements again.

She took off her shirt and yelled for Momin. When he came, she said, 'Momin, go next door, to number six and ask them for a tape measure. Tell them Shakeela needs it.'

21

Momin's gaze fell upon Shakila's white vest. He'd seen her this way many times before, but today it gave him a strange jolt. He averted his eyes, and anxiously said, 'What kind of measure, bibi?'

'A tape measure. This iron rod, lying in front of you, is one kind of measure. There is also another kind of measure, for clothes. Go and get it from number six, and run. Tell them Shakeela bibi needs it.'

Flat six was nearby. Momin returned in minutes with the tape measure. Shakeela took it from him and said, 'Wait here, for a second. You can take it back right away.' Then, addressing her sister, she said, 'These people, if you keep anything of theirs, they start plaguing you for it back. Here, will you take my measurements?'

Razia began measuring Shakeela's back and chest; they spoke continuously. Momin stood listening in the doorway, waiting out the uncomfortable silence.

'Razia, why don't you stretch it out and take the measurement. You did the same thing the last time. You took the measurements and the blouse was a mess. If it doesn't fit right in the front, it becomes baggy round the armpits.'

'Where to take it, where not to take it, you really give me a hard time. I start taking it in one place, you say, "a little lower". Is it the end of the world if it's a tiny bit too small or too big?'

'Yes, it is! It only looks good if it fits. Look at how well Surayya's clothes fit, do you ever see a crease? Do you see how good they look? Now, come on, get on with it.' With this, she took in a breath and pushed out her breasts.

22

When they were suitably enlarged, she held her breath and said, 'Come on, do it now, quickly.'

When Shakeela exhaled, Momin felt hundreds of balloons explode inside of him. He said nervously, 'Should I take it back, bibi, the tape?'

'Wait, one minute,' she replied dismissively.

As she said this, the clothes measure got entangled in her arms. When Shakeela tried disentangling it, Momin saw a tuft of black hair in her pale armpits. Similar hair had sprouted in his own armpits, but something about hers felt especially agreeable to him. A quiver ran through his entire body. He had a strange urge for this black hair to become his moustache. As a child, he would take black and golden corn hair and make moustaches from them. This urge now, gave him the same sensation round his nose and mouth that he had felt then, with the corn hair tickling against his upper lip.

Shakeela had lowered her arm and her armpit was hidden once again, but Momin still saw the tuft of black hair. The image of her raised arm, and the black hair poking out, remained fixed in his mind.

Shakeela handed Momin the measure and said, 'Go and give it back. And thank them profusely.'

Momin returned the measure and sat down in the house's courtyard. Dim thoughts rose in his mind. He sat at length considering their meaning but nothing became clear. Without intending to, he opened his little trunk, in which his newly tailored Eid clothes lay.

The smell of new cotton reached his nose, as the lid opened, and he felt the sudden urge to wash himself, put on his new clothes and go upstairs and salaam Shakeela

bibi. His new cotton salwar would crinkle and his fez…
No sooner had he thought of his fez than his gaze fell on
its tassel and this tassel was transformed into the tuft of
black hair he'd seen in Shakeela's armpits. He took out
his new fez from under his clothes and began to finger its
soft, bendy tassel when he heard Shakeela's voice.

'Momin!'

Momin put the hat back into the trunk, shut its lid
and went back to the room where Shakeela was working.
She had already cut many pieces of violet satin using her
sample. She put the pieces of bright, slippery cloth to
one side and turned to Momin. 'I called for you so many
times. Were you asleep?'

Momin became tongue-tied. 'No, bibi ji.'

'Then, what were you doing?'

'Nothing, nothing at all.'

'You must have been up to something.' Shakeela
assailed him with questions, but in fact her mind was
focussed on the blouse, on which she now had to put
preliminary stitches.

'I'd opened my trunk and was looking at my new
clothes,' Momin confessed with a forced laugh.

Hearing this, Shakeela laughed uproariously and
Razia joined in.

Seeing Shakeela laugh gave Momin a strangely
contented feeling and he wished at that moment to say
or do something funny, which would make Shakeela
laugh more. So, becoming coy, and taking on a girly
voice, he said, 'I'm also going to ask the mistress for
some money so that I can go off and get myself a silk
handkerchief.'

Still laughing, Shakeela asked, 'And what are you going to do with this handkerchief?'

'I'll tie it round my neck, bibi,' Momin said in his coy voice, 'it'll look so nice.'

Hearing this, Razia and Shakeela both laughed at length.

'If you tie it round your neck, don't forget I'll use it to hang you with.' Then, trying to suppress her laughter, she said to Razia, 'The cretin's made me forget what it was I called him for. What did I call him for?'

Razia didn't reply, but began humming a film song she'd been learning for the past two days. In the meantime, Shakeela remembered herself why she'd called him. 'Listen, Momin, I'm giving you this vest. Take it down to the new shop that's opened next to the chemist, the same one you went to with me the other day, and ask them how much six vests like this will cost. Be sure to tell them that I'll ask around and so they'd better give me a discount. Got it?'

'Yes, bibi,' Momin replied.

'Now leave the room.'

Momin stepped out of the door and a few moments later the vest landed near his feet. Shakeela's voice came from within: 'Tell them we want something just like it, the exact same design. There shouldn't be any difference.'

Momin said 'Very well' and picked up the vest, which had become slightly moist, as though it had been held over steam for a moment and pulled away. It was warm and sweet; the smell of her body still resided in it—and all this, was very pleasing to him.

Momin left, rubbing it between his fingers; it was as soft as a kitten. When he returned after enquiring about the prices, Shakeela had begun stitching her blouse, that violet satin blouse, far brighter and smoother than the tassel of his fez.

The blouse was perhaps being made in preparation for Eid, which was around the corner. Momin was called many times that day: to buy string, to take out the iron; the needle broke, to buy a new one. Shakeela put off the rest of the work till the next day, but pieces of string and scraps of violet satin were strewn about. Momin was called in to clear them away.

He cleared up well and threw everything away, except the shiny scraps of violet satin, which he saved for no particular reason.

The next day he took them out of his pocket and sat alone, taking apart their threads. He remained busy at this game until the little bits of string became a ball in his hand. He rubbed it and pressed it between his fingers, but Shakeela's armpit, in which he'd seen the clump of black hair, remained fixed in his mind.

He was summoned many times that day as well. He saw the violet satin blouse at every stage. When it was still rough, it had long, white stitches all over it. Then, it was ironed and its creases vanished and shine doubled. After this, while it still had its preliminary stitches, Shakeela tried it on and showed it to Razia. In the dressing table mirror in the other room, she saw how it looked from every angle. When she was satisfied, she took it off, making markings wherever it was tight or loose. Then, she corrected its imperfections and tried it on once again. Only when it fit perfectly did she begin the final stitching.

On one hand, the blouse was being stitched, on the other, strange and troubling thoughts came loose in Momin's mind. When he was called into the room, and his gaze fell on the bright satin blouse, he'd feel the urge to touch, not just to touch, but to caress its soft, silky surface with his rough fingers.

He had felt its softness from the scraps of satin. The threads he had saved had become softer still. When he'd made a ball of these threads, he discovered while pressing them that they had something of the texture of rubber as well. Whenever he'd come in and see the blouse, his mind would race towards the hair he had seen in Shakeela's armpits. Would it also be soft like the satin, he wondered?

The blouse was ready at last. Momin was wiping the floor with a damp cloth when Shakeela entered. She took off her shirt and put it on the bed. Under it, she wore a white vest, exactly like the one Momin had taken to enquire the price of. She put on her hand-stitched blouse over it, did up its hooks and went to stand in front of the mirror.

Momin, still wiping the floor, looked up at the mirror. A new life had come into the blouse; in one or two places it gleamed so brightly that it looked as if the satin had turned white. Shakeela had her back to Momin, and the long curve and full depth of her spine were visible because of the close fit of the blouse. Momin could no longer contain himself.

He said, 'Bibi, you've even outdone the tailors!'

She was pleased to hear herself praised, but impatient for Razia's opinion, and only said, 'It's nice, isn't it?' before running out of the door. Momin was left gazing at the mirror, in which the blouse's dark and bright reflection lingered for a while.

At night when he went into the room again to leave a jug of water, he saw the blouse hanging from a wooden hanger. No one else was in the room. He took a few steps forward and looked intently at the blouse. Then, full of trepidation, he ran his hand over it. It made him feel as though someone was running their hand, as lightly as breeze, over the downy hairs on his body.

That night he had many restless dreams. The deputy saab's wife ordered him to smash a great heap of coal, but when he struck it with the hammer, it became a soft tuft of hair. Which were really the fine strands of a ball of spun black sugar. Then, these balls turned into many black balloons and began to fly up into the air. They went very high before starting to burst. The sky thundered and the tassel of Momin's fez went missing. He went out in search of it. He wandered from place to place. The smell of fresh cotton greeted him from somewhere. He didn't know what happened next. His hand fell on a black satin blouse. He ran it for some time over a throbbing object. Suddenly, he got up. For a while he couldn't understand what had happened. Then, he felt fear, surprise and a pang. He was in a strange state. He was aware at first of a warm pain; but moments later, a cool ripple travelled through his body.

Khol Do

The special train left Amritsar at two in the afternoon and reached Mughalpura eight hours later. Many people were killed en route, many injured; some went astray.

Ten am. Old Sirajuddin opened his eyes on the cold floor of the camp; seeing the swelling sea of men, women and children, he became still more confused. He stared vacantly at the murky sky. There was chaos all round him, but he heard nothing, as if his ears were blocked. Anyone who saw him would think he was consumed by deep worry. But that was not so: his nerves were frayed; he felt as if he were floating in a void.

His eyes struck the sun, and he awoke with a start as its sharp blaze entered him. Images assailed from all sides. Loot. Fire. Stampede. Station. Bullets. Night. And Sakina. Sirajuddin stood up immediately, and like a madman, began surveying the sea of people all round him.

For three full hours he scoured the camp, crying, 'Sakina, Sakina.' But he learned nothing of the whereabouts of his only daughter. All round him, there was mayhem. Someone looked for his son, another for his mother; someone for his wife, another for his daughter. Sirajuddin, tired and defeated, sat down on one side and tried to recall where and when he had been separated from Sakina. But as he racked his brains, his mind fixed on Sakina's mother's body, her intestines spilled out, then he could think no further.

Sakina's mother was dead. She had taken her last breath before Sirajuddin's eyes. But where was Sakina?

Her mother had said as she was dying, 'Let me be. Take Sakina and run.'

Sakina had been at his side. They had both run barefoot. Sakina's dupatta had fallen down. He had stopped to pick it up, but Sakina screamed, 'Abbaji, leave it!' But he had picked it up anyway. His eyes fell on his coat as he remembered this. He put his hand in the bulging pocket and took out a cloth: Sakina's dupatta! But where was Sakina?

Sirajuddin tried hard to remember, but to no avail. Had he brought Sakina as far as the station? Had she boarded the train with him? Had he become unconscious when the train was stopped, and the rioters came aboard? Was that how they were able to make off with Sakina?

Sirajuddin's mind was full of questions, but not a single answer. He was in need of comfort, but then so were all the people scattered round him. Sirajuddin wanted to cry, but his eyes would not cooperate. Who knew where all the tears had gone?

Six days later, once his nerves had settled, Sirajuddin met eight young men. They had a lorry and guns and said they would help him. Sirajuddin blessed them over and over again and gave them a description of Sakina. 'She's fair and very beautiful; she's taken after her mother, not me. She's about seventeen. Large eyes, black hair, there's a big beauty spot on her right cheek. She's my only daughter. Please find her. Your God will reward you.'

The young volunteers assured old Sirajuddin, with great feeling, that if his daughter was alive, she would be by his side within a few days.

The men made every effort, even putting their lives on the line. They went to Amritsar and rescued men, women and children, and brought them to safety. Ten days passed, but Sakina was not to be found.

One day, the men were driving to Amritsar in their lorry, engaged in their work when, near Cherat*, they saw a girl on the side of the road. She gave a start at the sound of the lorry and began to run. The volunteers turned off the engine and ran after her, managing to catch her in a field. She was very beautiful, with a large beauty spot on her right cheek. One of the men asked, 'Are you Sakina?'

The girl's face became pale. She didn't reply. It was only after the men had reassured her that her terror left her, and she confessed she was Sirajuddin's daughter, Sakina.

The eight young volunteers comforted her, sat her in their lorry and gave her food and milk. She was distressed to be without a dupatta, and tried vainly to cover her breasts with her arms until one of the men took off his coat and gave it to her.

Many days passed. Sirajuddin still had no news of Sakina. He would spend the whole day doing rounds of the different camps and offices, but received no word about Sakina's whereabouts. At night he would pray for the success of the young men. They had assured him that if Sakina was alive, they would find her within a few days.

One day Sirajuddin saw the young volunteers at the camp. They were sitting in the lorry. Sirajuddin ran up to them. The lorry was about to head out when

---

* A town in the North West Frontier Province.

Sirajuddin asked, 'Boys, have you heard anything about my Sakina?'

They all said in one voice, 'We will, we will.' And the lorry drove away. Sirajuddin prayed once again for their success and his heart was a little lighter.

Towards evening, there was a disturbance in the camp near where Sirajuddin sat. Four men were bringing something in. He made enquiries and discovered that a girl had been found unconscious near the rail tracks; she was being brought in now. Sirajuddin set off behind them. The people handed her over to the hospital and left.

Sirajuddin stood still outside the hospital beside a wooden pole. Then slowly, he went in. There was no one in the dark room, just a stretcher with a body on it. Sirajuddin approached, taking small steps. Suddenly, the room lit up. Sirajuddin saw a mole on the pale face of the body, and cried, 'Sakina!'

The doctor who had turned on the lights said to Sirajuddin, 'What is it?'

Sirajuddin managed only to say, 'Sir, I'm... sir, I'm... I'm her father.'

The doctor looked at the body on the stretcher. He checked its pulse and said to Sirajuddin, 'The window, open it!'

At the sound of the words, Sakina's corpse moved. Her dead hands undid her salwar and lowered it. Old Sirajuddin cried with happiness, 'She's alive, my daughter's alive!'

The doctor was drenched from head to toe in sweat.

Khaled Mian

Mumtaz had taken to rising early and sweeping all three rooms of his house. He made sure he removed cigarette butts, burnt matchsticks and things of this kind from every nook and cranny in the house. When all three rooms had been cleaned, he breathed a sigh of satisfaction.

His wife was asleep outside in the courtyard. The child was in his crib.

The reason Mumtaz had taken to rising early and sweeping the house's three rooms himself was that his son, Khaled, had just started walking. And, like all children at that age, he picked up whatever came his way and put it in his mouth.

It never failed to surprise Mumtaz that despite cleaning the entire house himself every day, and with great care, Khaled, his firstborn who was not yet a year old, would always find something or the other—a flake of plaster with dirt and dust sticking to it—to pick up with his tiny nails.

Mumtaz had become obsessed with cleanliness. If ever he saw Khaled pick something up off the floor and put it in his mouth, he would chide himself with all his heart—why had he been so careless?

He didn't love Khaled; he adored him. But as Khaled's first birthday approached, Mumtaz felt a dark fear grow into something of a conviction that his son would die before he was one.

He had mentioned this foreboding to his wife. Mumtaz was famous for not believing in such superstitions. So when his wife first heard of it, she said, 'You? And these kinds of fears? By God's goodwill, our son will live to be a hundred. I've made arrangements for his first birthday that will leave you speechless.'

Hearing this, Mumtaz felt a kind of jolt in his heart. Of course he wanted his son to live, but how could he rid himself of his fear?

Khaled was in excellent health. One day in winter, after he had returned from taking Khaled for a walk, the servant said to Mumtaz's wife, 'Begum saab, you mustn't put rouge on Khaled mian's cheeks; someone will put the evil eye on him.' His wife laughed loudly when she heard this. 'You fool, what need is there for me to put rouge on his cheeks when, mashallah, they are naturally so red?'

In winter, Khaled's cheeks had been red, but now in summer, they seemed somewhat sallow. He was very fond of water. Before going to the office, Mumtaz would stand him in a bucket of water. Khaled would stay there at length, splashing about and spraying water all around him. It made Mumtaz and his wife very happy to see him, except that with Mumtaz now, his happiness was obscured by a cloud of sadness. He would think, 'God, may my wife be right! Why am I possessed with this fear of his death? Why has this dread that he will die crept into my heart? Why will he die? He's a happy, healthy kid, many times healthier than other kids his age. I must be going mad. It's my excessive love for this child that's causing this fear. But why do I love him so much? Do all fathers love their children in this way? Does every father live with the fear that his child will die? What the hell has happened to me?'

34

After Mumtaz had swept all three rooms thoroughly, he liked to put a mat on the floor and lie down. After sweeping, especially in the summer, he would rest for half an hour without a pillow. This was how he relaxed.

Lying down today, he thought, 'The day after tomorrow is my child's first birthday. If it passes safely, without incident, I know the weight on my chest will lift. My fears will become a distant thing. O God, it's all in your hands.'

His eyes were closed when suddenly he felt a weight land on his bare chest. He opened his eyes to find it was Khaled. His wife stood nearby. She said that Khaled had been restless all night; he had shivered in his sleep as though from fear; he now lay trembling on Mumtaz's chest. Placing his hand on him, Mumtaz said, 'God, be my son's protector.'

His wife's voice rose with anger, 'God forbid! You're consumed by these fears. It's only a light fever, you know. God willing, it will go.'

She said this and left the room. Very gently, and with great love, Mumtaz began to stroke Khaled, who lay face down on his chest, shivering from time to time in his sleep. The stroking woke Khaled. He opened his big black eyes slowly and smiled when he saw his father. Mumtaz kissed him. 'What's the matter, Khaled. Why are you trembling?' Khaled dropped his head on his father's chest. Mumtaz began to stroke him lightly again. Silently, and with all his heart, he prayed that his son would live long.

His wife had made big preparations for Khaled's first birthday. She had invited all her friends. She had had the tailor stitch clothes especially for the birthday. The menu and a great deal more had already been planned. Mumtaz didn't like all this pomp. He would have preferred for no one to know, and for the birthday to pass, and for his son to turn one even without him remembering it. He only wanted to be aware of it once Khaled was a few days past the one year mark.

Khaled rose from his father's chest. Mumtaz, his voice filled with affection, said, 'Khaled, won't you get up and greet your father?'

Khaled smiled, and raising his hand, touched it to his forehead. Mumtaz blessed him. 'May you live long.' But as soon as he said it, he felt that painful foreboding in his heart again, and felt himself submerged in a sea of sorrow.

Khaled went out of the room. There was still some time before Mumtaz had to leave for the office. He continued to lie on the mat, determined to ease the dread in his heart and mind. Suddenly, he heard his wife's alarmed voice in the courtyard: 'Mumtaz saab, Mumtaz saab! Come here!'

Mumtaz rose with a start and ran out. His wife stood outside the bathroom, holding Khaled, who twisted and turned in her arms. Mumtaz took Khaled into his arms and demanded to know what had happened. His wife, her voice thick with fear, said, 'I don't know. He was playing in the water. I was cleaning his nose and he suddenly had a fit.'

Khaled twisted in Mumtaz's arms as though someone was squeezing him like a piece of wet cloth. Mumtaz laid him down on the bed; both husband and wife were gripped by terror. Khaled lay shaking and the two of them, half out of their wits, didn't know if they should caress him, kiss him or sprinkle water on him. His convulsions just wouldn't subside.

After some time, when the fit did subside, and Khaled lost consciousness, Mumtaz believed he had died. Turning to his wife, he said quietly, 'He's gone.'

'The devil be cursed!' she shrieked. 'What things come out of your mouth? He's had a convulsion—it's over; he'll be fine any minute now.'

Khaled opened his large, black eyes, now tired and drooping, and looked at his father. Mumtaz's world revived. 'Khaled, my son, what was that? What happened to you?' he asked anxiously. A wan smile appeared on Khaled's face. Mumtaz lifted him up in his arms and took him into the room. He was about to lay him down when the second convulsion came. Again, Khaled started to twist and turn as though seized by an epileptic fit. So strong was this convulsion that Mumtaz felt that instead of Khaled, he himself was in its grip.

The second fit ended; Khaled wilted further. His big black eyes were sunken. Mumtaz began talking to him.

'Khaled, my son, what is this that keeps happening to you?'

'Khaled mian, get up, no? Move about.'

'Will Khaled have some butter?'

Khaled loved butter, but even this evoked no reaction. When Mumtaz asked if he'd have his favourite sweets, he weakly shook his head to say no. Mumtaz smiled and clutched him to his chest. Then handing him over to his wife, he said, 'Take care of him. I'm going to go and get a doctor.'

When he returned with the doctor, he found his wife out of her wits. In his absence, Khaled had had three more fits. They had left him almost lifeless. But the doctor saw Khaled and said that there was no cause for worry. 'Children routinely have convulsions of this kind. It's because they're teething, and sometimes, if there are worms in the stomach, that can also be a cause. I'll write you a prescription; it'll give him some rest. His fever's not high. You mustn't worry at all.'

Mumtaz took the day off from work and sat by Khaled's side all day. After the doctor left, the child had two more fits. After that he lay there unmoving. By evening, Mumtaz thought, 'Perhaps now we've seen God's mercy. There have been no convulsions for quite some time. May the Lord let the night pass like this too.'

Mumtaz's wife was relieved too. 'If the Lord wishes it, tomorrow my Khaled will be up and running about.' Khaled had to be given his medicine at fixed times through the night. Out of fear of falling asleep, Mumtaz didn't lie down in bed, but put an armchair near Khaled's crib and sat up. He stayed up all night as Khaled was restless. He would tremble and wake up repeatedly; his fever was high too.

In the morning, when Mumtaz took Khaled's temperature, it was a hundred and four degrees. The doctor was called. He said, 'There's no cause for worry. He has bronchitis. I'll write out a prescription. He'll feel better in three or four days.'

The doctor wrote out the prescription and left. Mumtaz had the medicine prepared. He gave Khaled one dose, but Khaled did not feel any better. At about ten o'clock,

Mumtaz called a more renowned doctor. He examined Khaled closely and reassured them, saying there was no cause for concern. Everything would be fine.

Everything was not fine. The renowned doctor's medicine had no effect; Khaled's fever continued to rise. Mumtaz's servant said, 'Saab, this is no illness. Khaled mian has come under someone's evil eye. I'll go and have a protective charm made. By God's will, it'll take effect.'

Sacred water from seven wells was collected. The charm was dissolved in it and given to Khaled. It had no effect. A neighbour came over. She prescribed a Unani medicine; Mumtaz went out and bought it, but in the end didn't give it to Khaled. In the evening, a relative of Mumtaz's came over and brought another doctor with him. The doctor looked at Khaled and said he had malaria. 'The fever only ever gets so high when it's malaria. Give an ice water compress; I'll give him a quinine injection.'

With the cold compress, the fever instantly came down to ninety eight degrees. Mumtaz and his wife were relieved, but soon it rose even higher. Mumtaz took Khaled's temperature; it had risen to a hundred and six degrees.

The neighbour came, and looking gloomily at Khaled, said to Mumtaz, 'I am sure the vertebrae in his neck have broken.'

Mumtaz and his wife's spirits sank. Mumtaz called the hospital from the warehouse below. The hospital asked him to bring the patient across. Mumtaz sent for a horse carriage, and taking Khaled in his arms, set out with his wife for the hospital. Mumtaz had been drinking water all day, but he was still thirsty. On the way to the hospital, his throat became unbearably parched. He thought he would stop in a shop and have a glass of water. But, God knows from where, a sense of foreboding suddenly took hold of him. 'Look, if you drink water,' it seemed to say, 'your Khaled will die.'

Mumtaz's throat became bone dry, but he didn't drink any water. When the carriage came near the hospital, he lit a cigarette. He had taken only two drags when he suddenly threw it away. A thought echoed in his mind: 'Mumtaz, don't smoke a cigarette; your child will die.' Mumtaz stopped the carriage; he thought, 'What is this stupidity? These fears are futile; what calamity can come to the child from my smoking a cigarette?'

He got off the carriage and picked up the cigarette from the street. He had got back into the carriage, and was just about to take a drag, when some unknown power stopped him. 'No, Mumtaz, don't do this; Khaled will die.'

Mumtaz violently threw the cigarette away. The coachman stared wide-eyed at him. Mumtaz felt he could read his mind and was mocking him. He said defensively, 'It was bad, the cigarette.' Saying this, he took a new cigarette out of his pocket. He wanted to light it, but was scared. His mind was in turmoil: his reason told him that his superstitions were futile, but another voice, another power, overran his logic.

The carriage went through the hospital gates and Mumtaz put the cigarette out with his fingers and threw it away. He felt wretched at the thought of being enslaved by his fears. The men at the hospital admitted Khaled immediately. The doctor looked at Khaled and said, 'It's bronchial pneumonia; his condition is critical.'

Khaled was unconscious. His mother sat at the head of his bed looking at him, her eyes filled with despair. The room had an attached bathroom. Mumtaz felt great thirst. He turned on the tap and started to drink from his cupped hand when that same dread returned to his mind: 'Mumtaz, what are you doing? Don't drink water. Your Khaled will die.'

Mumtaz ignored his fear and drank so much water that his stomach bloated. Once he'd quenched his thirst, he came out of the bathroom into the room where Khaled lay, withered and unconscious on the hospital's iron bed. Mumtaz wanted to escape; to lose consciousness; for Khaled to recover and for the pneumonia to take hold of him instead.

Mumtaz noticed that Khaled was paler than before. He thought, 'This is all the result of my having drunk water… If I hadn't drunk water, Khaled's condition would definitely have improved.' He felt terrible remorse. He cursed himself, but even as he did so, he felt that the person thinking these thoughts was not him, but somebody else. Who was this somebody else? Why did this person's mind manufacture these fears? He was thirsty; he drank water. What effect could that have on Khaled? Khaled would surely recover. Day after tomorrow was his birthday. God willing, it would be celebrated with great pomp.

But presently his heart sank. A voice told him that Khaled would not live to turn one. Mumtaz wished he could tear its tongue from the root. But the voice came

41

from no place other than his own mind; Lord knows how it came and why.

Tormented by his fears, Mumtaz remonstrated with himself: 'For God's sake, have mercy on me! Why have you chosen a poor soul like me to cling to?'

Evening fell. Many doctors had examined Khaled. Medicines had been given; many injections administered, but Khaled remained unconscious. All of a sudden, a voice rang in Mumtaz's head, telling him to leave the hospital room, to go away immediately or Khaled would die.

Mumtaz went out of the room. He left the hospital. The voice continued to ring in his head. He gave in to it, his every movement, his every action surrendered to its will. It took him into a hotel. It told him to drink alcohol. The alcohol came; it ordered him to throw it away. Mumtaz threw the glass from his hand; the voice told him to order more. A second glass came; it told him to throw this away too.

After paying the bill for the alcohol and the broken glasses, Mumtaz went outside. Everywhere there seemed to be silence and more silence. In his mind alone, there was clamour. He arrived back at the hospital and headed for Khaled's room, but the voice spoke: 'Don't go there, Mumtaz. Khaled will die.'

He turned around. There was a bench in a grassy maidan. He lay down on it. It was ten at night. The maidan was dark and silent. Sometimes the horn of a car would graze the silence as it went past. Up ahead, over a high wall, the illuminated hospital clock could be seen. Mumtaz thought of Khaled. 'Will he survive? Why are children who are meant to die born in the first place?

42

Why is that life born that has to go so quickly into the mouth of death? Khaled will definitely… '

That instant, he felt a rush of fear and fell to his knees. The voice ordered him to remain in this position until Khaled recovered. Mumtaz remained prostrate. He wanted to say a prayer, but was told not to. His eyes filled with tears. He prayed not for Khaled, but for himself. 'God, free me from this ordeal! If you want to kill Khaled, then kill Khaled! What torment is this?'

Then he heard a noise. Some distance away, two men were sitting on chairs, eating and talking amongst themselves.

'Such a beautiful kid.'

'I can't bear to see the mother.'

'The poor thing, she falls at the feet of every doctor.'

'We've done every possible thing on our end.'

'It'll be difficult to save him.'

'I said to the mother, "You have to pray, sister."'

One doctor looked towards Mumtaz, who was still prostrate on his knees. He yelled loudly, 'Hey, what are you doing there? Come here!'

Mumtaz rose and approached the doctors. One asked, 'Who are you?'

Mumtaz, running his tongue over his dry lips, said, 'Sir, I am a patient.'

'If you're a patient,' the doctor replied harshly, 'then you must go inside. Why are you in the maidan doing squats?'

Mumtaz replied, 'Sir, my boy… is in that ward over there.'

'That's your child who…'

'Yes, perhaps it was him you were speaking of. He's my son. Khaled.'

'You're his father?'

Mumtaz nodded his tormented head, 'Yes, I am his father.'

The doctor said, 'And you're sitting here? Go upstairs. Your wife is beside herself!'

'Yes, sir,' Mumtaz said and went towards the ward. He climbed the stairs and saw his servant outside the room, crying. When the servant saw Mumtaz, he cried even harder. 'Saab, Khaled mian is no more.'

Mumtaz entered the room. His wife was lying there, unconscious. A doctor and a nurse were trying to revive her. Mumtaz went and stood by the bed. Khaled lay there with his eyes closed. Death's peacefulness was apparent on his face. Mumtaz stroked his silky hair, and in a choking voice, said, 'Will you have a sweet?'

Khaled did not move his head to say no. Mumtaz implored him, 'Khaled mian, will you take my fears away with you?'

Mumtaz thought Khaled nodded his head in assent.

My Name is Radha

This story is from the days when there wasn't so much as a hint of the present war. It happened some eight or nine years ago, when, unlike today, even life's upheavals came in an orderly fashion.

I was employed at the time with a film studio, earning forty rupees a month, and my life moved at an even, happy pace. I'd arrive at the studio around ten, give Nayaz Muhammad Villain's cat two paise worth of milk, write B-grade dialogues for a B-grade movie, joke a little with the Bengali actress who, in those days, was called Bulbul Bangal, then suck up to Dada Gore, who was the biggest film director at the time, and finally make my way home.

The studio owner Harmzji Framji, a fat, red-cheeked bon vivant of sorts, was madly in love with a middle aged actress who looked like a transvestite. His favourite pastime was sizing up the breasts of every newly arrived actress. Another Muslim hooker from Calcutta's Bow Bazaar carried on affairs simultaneously with her director, sound recordist and scriptwriter. The point of these affairs of course, was to ensure that all three remained in love with her.

The Beauty of the Forest was being shot at the time. And it was for this film that, after feeding Nayaz Muhammad Villain's wild cats—which he'd bred in order to create heaven knows what effect on the crew—two paise worth of milk, I would write dialogue as if in another tongue; for I knew nothing of what the film's story or plot was. At the time, I was a mere clerk whose job it was to stand with a pencil and paper, noting down whatever was said, wrong or right, in Urdu that director saab could understand.

But, anyway! *The Beauty of the Forest* was being shot and a rumour had begun to circulate that Harmzji Framji was bringing a new face onto the set for the role of the vamp. The part of the hero had already been given to Raj Kishore.

Raj Kishore was a handsome, well-built young man from Rawalpindi. People generally thought that his physique was manly and attractive. I thought about this often, and though his body was certainly athletic and proportionate, I could never see the attraction. This might well be because I, myself thin and weedy, generally favour people of my own body type.

That's not to say that I hated Raj Kishore; I've hated very few people in my life; but I didn't like him much. I'd like to reveal my reasons to you gradually.

Raj Kishore's accent and manner of speaking, which were typical of Rawalpindi, I adored. If ever there is beauty and music to be found in Punjabi, it is to be found in the language spoken in Rawalpindi. The language of that city is at once masculine and feminine, both sweet and textured. When a woman from Rawalpindi speaks to you, it's like the taste of a ripe mango's juices flooding your mouth... It wasn't mangoes I was speaking of though, but Raj Kishore, of whom I was considerably less fond.

As I said before, he was a handsome, well-built young man. If the matter had ended there, I would have had no objection. The problem was that he, Kishore that is, was only too aware of his good looks and physique, a vanity which I find insufferable.

To be well-built is one thing but to foist it on everyone else like an illness is quite another. And Raj Kishore was badly afflicted with this disease. He was always trying to impress those smaller and weaker than him with an unnecessary show of his physique.

There's no doubt that I myself am sickly and weak; one of my lungs can barely draw air; but God be my witness, I have never once advertised this weakness. I'm aware that men can profit from their weaknesses no less than they can from their strengths, but I believe it's wrong to do so. Beauty, for me, is something to be praised quietly, not loudly and garishly.

Too much good health can also come to seem like an illness. And Raj Kishore, though he possessed all the beauty a young man can possess, was in the habit of making a vulgar exhibition of it. He'd be talking to you, and at the same time, flexing a bicep. A serious discussion could be going on, say about independence, and he'd stand there, the buttons of his khadi kurta open, measuring the width of his chest.

The mention of his khadi kurta reminds me that Raj Kishore was an ardent Congress supporter. This was why he wore khadi, and yet I always suspected he didn't love his country nearly as much as he loved himself.

Many would feel that my description of Raj Kishore was unfair. Everyone, in and out of the studio, was an admirer of his body, his opinions, his simplicity and of course, his distinctive, Rawalpindi style of speaking.

Unlike the other actors, Raj Kishore was neither aloof nor unapproachable. If the Congress staged a demonstration, he would certainly be there. If there was a literary gathering, he was sure to be present. He even took time out from his busy schedule to be there for his neighbours and acquaintances when they were in trouble.

All the film producers respected him because the purity of his character was well known. Forget film producers, even the public knew that Raj Kishore was a man of moral fibre. And for any man to be part of the film world and remain free from the taint of scandal, is no small achievement. Raj Kishore was a successful actor, but it was these unique qualities that placed him on an even higher pedestal.

In the evenings, outside the paan shop in Nagpara, talk would invariably turn to the lives of actors and actresses. Virtually each one had some scandal or another linked to their name, but whenever Raj Kishore's name came up, Sham Lal, the paanwallah, would say with great pride: 'Manto saab, Raj bhai is one actor who knows to keep his dick in his trousers.'

How he'd come to call him 'Raj bhai', I don't know. But it didn't surprise me. Even the most ordinary things about 'Raj bhai' were turned into great feats and reached the ears of ordinary people. They knew how he spent his income—what he sent to his father; what he donated to orphanages; what he kept for himself—as if they'd been made to learn it by heart.

Sham Lal told me one day that Raj bhai had very good relations with his stepmother. In the days when he had no money, his father and his new wife had tormented

him constantly, but it was to his credit that when the
time came, he did his duty by them, providing them
with a comfortable life. They now slept on big beds,
lording over people. Every morning, Raj went and saw
his stepmother, even touching her feet. He stood with
folded hands before his father and gave him anything
he asked for. Now don't take it amiss, but I'd become
irritated whenever I heard Raj Kishore praised in this
way. God, alone, knows why!

As I've said before, I didn't really hate him. He never
gave me any reason to. And in that time when clerks were
given no respect, he often sat for hours talking to me. So
I can't say that there was a reason, but a doubt, which
had all the force of a conviction, struck like lightning
in a dark corner of my mind, telling me that Raj was
posturing; that his entire life was somehow fraudulent.
The problem was that I couldn't find anyone of the same
mind as me—people worshipped him like a god—and
this bothered me deeply.

Raj had a wife and four children; he was a good
husband and a good father; there was no corner of
this stainless cover that could be lifted to reveal a dark
element in his life.

He was everything he appeared to be. And yet, I was
racked with doubt.

Believe me, I chided myself on many occasions. I felt I
must truly be perverse for harbouring suspicions about a
man the whole world thought so well of and who I, myself,
had no cause for complaint about. What did it matter that
he admired his own admittedly attractive physique? If I had
such a physique, I would in all likelihood do the same.

But I was never able to come round to seeing Raj Kishore the way others did and was often nettled by him. He'd say something I didn't like and I'd pounce on him. Our bouts would invariably end with him smiling and me, left with a bad taste in my mouth, more troubled than ever.

There wasn't a hint of scandal in his life. Besides his wife's, no other woman's clean or dirty laundry could be linked to his name. I should also mention that he referred to all the other actresses as 'sister'; and they, in turn, referred to him as 'brother'. This only raised more questions in my mind. Why was it necessary to establish these intimacies? A brother and sister's relationship was something apart; why call all women your sisters as if you were putting up a 'Road Closed' or 'It Is Forbidden to Urinate Here' sign?

If you weren't planning on having a sexual relationship with a woman, why make an announcement? If no thought of a woman other than your wife could enter your mind, why run an advertisement about it? I couldn't understand it and this upset me.

But, anyway! *The Beauty of the Forest*'s shooting continued; the studio was especially busy; women extras came regularly and our day would be spent laughing and joking with them.

One morning, the makeup artist who we called Ustad arrived in Nayaz Muhammad Villain's room with news that the new girl, meant to be playing the part of the vamp, had arrived and was to begin work imminently. We were on a break at the time, and the effect of hot tea along with this little bit of news fired us up. The arrival of a new girl in the studio was always cause for commotion. And so we emptied out of Nayaz Muhammad Villain's and set off in the hope of catching a glimpse of her.

In the evening, at the time when Harmzji Framji left his office for the billiards room, pressing two fragranced paans from Isa the tabla player's silver box into his wide cheek, we caught sight of the girl.

She was dark-skinned; and that was all I was able to discern. She was shaking hands with a businessman, then hurriedly got into the studio car and drove away. I ran into Nayaz Muhammad a few moments later, who was only able to say that she had thick lips; that was perhaps all he had been able to see of her. Ustad, who might not have even seen that much, shook his head and grunted, 'Hoonh... Condemn,' which meant bullshit.

Four or five days passed, but the new girl didn't appear at the studio. On the fifth or sixth day, as I was leaving Gulab's Hotel after a cup of tea, I ran straight into her.

I have always preferred to observe women furtively, with sidelong glances. If a woman appears suddenly, and directly, in front of me, I'm unable to make her out. And because we ran straight into one another, I wasn't able to discern her face or features. I did, however, see her feet, on which she wore fashionable new slippers.

The studio's owners had gravelled the path that led from the laboratory to the studio. There were countless small round pebbles, on which the shoe routinely slipped. And because her slippers were open, she walked with some difficulty.

But after this meeting, my friendship with Ms Neelam began gradually to grow. The studio people knew nothing of it, even though we came to be on fairly informal terms, and really quite close. Her real name was Radha. I once asked her why she had dropped such a pretty name. 'Just like that,' she replied, then a moment later, added, 'It's such a pretty name that I wouldn't want it to end up in a film.'

This remark might perhaps make you think that Radha was religious. Not in the slightest; she had no feeling whatsoever for religion and its superstitions. But just as I, before beginning any new writing, always inscribe the numerals denoting Bismillah—7, 8, 6—on the page, she had, even perhaps without meaning to, a special affection for the name Radha.

Since she preferred to go by Neelam, I will refer to her from hereon as that.

Neelam was the daughter of a Banarasi prostitute*. She spoke in the accent of that region, which is very pleasing to the ears. My name is Saadat, but she always referred to me as Sadaq. I once said to her, 'Neelam, I know you can say Saadat so I don't understand why you won't correct yourself?' When she heard this, a faint smile rose to her dark lips, which were in fact very thin. She replied, 'The mistakes I make once, I don't usually put right.'

I don't think many people in the studio were aware that the woman they took to be an ordinary actress possessed such idiosyncrasies. She wasn't hustling like the other actresses. Her seriousness, which every man in the studio misconstrued, was in fact, a very endearing thing.

It suited her, like rouge on her dark, clear skin. And the sadness that had settled in her eyes and the

---

* The word in Urdu is tawwaif, which covers anything from a working prostitute to a dancing girl or courtesan.

corners of her mouth set her even further apart from the other women.

I was—and still am—astonished that she had been chosen for the role of the vamp in *The Beauty of the Forest*; she didn't seem at all fast or wanton. It was painful to see her for the first time on the set in the tight bodice she had to wear for her odious part. She was very good at sensing the reactions of others, and so upon seeing me, said immediately: 'Director saab was saying, because your part isn't that of a decent woman, you have been given these clothes to wear. I said, "If these are clothes, I might as well walk naked with you onto the set."'

'And what did the director say to that?'

A faint smile appeared on Neelam's thin lips. She said, 'He began imagining me naked. What fools, these people are! Dressed as I am, what need is there for the poor wretches to leave anything to the imagination!'

As far as her sharp-wittedness went, little more need be said. But I want now to come to those incidents that will help me complete this story.

The rains in Bombay begin as early as June and continue until the middle of September. The rain in the first two, two and a half months, is such that work in the studio becomes impossible. The shooting of *The Beauty of the Forest* began in the last week of April. And when the first rain came, we were just about to complete our third set. Only one small scene remained, and as it had no dialogue, we were able to continue our work despite the rain. But when this was finished, we were put out of action for a period.

The studio crew had a lot of time to sit around and

chat with each other. I'd spend whole days at Gulab's Hotel, drinking tea. Everyone who came in was either partially or entirely drenched. The flies too, seeking shelter from the rain, collected within. It was squalid beyond words. A squeezed rag for making tea was draped on one chair; on another, lay a foul smelling knife, used for cutting onions, but now idle. Gulab saab stood nearby, devouring Bombay Urdu with his meat eating teeth: 'I, there, not going... I going from here... there'll be a big bust-up... O, yes, the shit is bound to hit the fan.' Except for Harmzji Framji, his brother-in-law, Eedelji and the heroines, everyone came to Gulab's Hotel, with its corrugated steel roof. Nayaz Muhammad, of course, came several times a day as he was rearing two cats called Chunni and Munni.

Raj Kishore did the rounds once a day as well. As soon as his large, athletic frame appeared in the doorway, everyone's eyes, save mine, brightened. The young male actors would jump up and offer their chairs. Once he'd sat down, they'd settle around him like moths. After this, one would hear praise of Raj Kishore's past performances, which was ready on the lips of the male extras. Then from Raj Kishore himself, we would hear the history of his leaving school for college, and from college entering the world of film. I already knew all of this by heart, and would say my hellos and goodbyes as soon as he entered, then make for the door.

One afternoon, when the rain let up and Harmzji Framji's Alsatian, after being frightened off by Nayaz Muhammad's cats, came bounding in the direction of Gulab's Hotel, with his tail between his legs, I saw Neelam and Raj Kishore talking under a maulsari*. Raj Kishore was standing, swinging lightly, which he often did when by his own estimation, he was making riveting conversation. I can't recall when or how Neelam met Raj Kishore, but she had known him before she entered the film world and might even have praised his well-proportioned, attractive body to me once or twice in passing.

I had left Gulab's Hotel and gone as far as the porch of the recording room when I saw Raj Kishore swing a khadi bag off his wide shoulders and take out a thick notebook. I understood; this was Raj Kishore's diary.

Every day Raj Kishore, having finished his work and taken his stepmother's blessings, would write faithfully in his diary before going to bed. Though he loved Punjabi, he chose English for these daily entries, in which it was possible to see, here traces of Tagore's delicate style, there of Gandhi's political prose. There was even something of the influence of Shakespeare's plays on his writing. But I never saw in this amalgam, anything of the writer's own true self. Should this diary ever fall into your hands, you will know everything of Raj Kishore's life over the last ten or fifteen years: how many rupees he gave to charity; how much he spent on feeding the poor; how many demonstrations he attended, what he wore, what he took off. And if my guess is right, on some page of this diary my name will appear next to 'thirty five rupees', which I once borrowed from Raj Kishore and haven't returned to date, only because I'm certain the money's repayment will never be recorded in the diary.

Anyway! He was reading some pages from this diary to

---

* Spanish cherry tree

Neelam. I could tell from a distance, from the movement of his beautiful lips, that he was praising the Lord in Shakespearean style. Neelam sat in silence on the round, cemented platform under the maulsari. Raj Kishore's words seemed to be having no effect on her.

She was looking instead at his puffed up chest. The buttons of his kurta were open, and against his pale skin, his black chest hair looked especially attractive.

The studio had been washed clean. Even Nayaz Muhammad's cats, who were normally filthy, were immaculate today. They both sat on an adjacent bench cleaning their faces with their soft paws. Neelam was dressed in a spotless white georgette sari. Her blouse was of white linen and it produced the gentlest, most pleasing contrast against her dark, rounded arms.

Why did she look so different?

For a moment, the question took root in my mind. When our eyes met a moment later, the disquiet in them answered my question. She was in love. She gestured to me to come over. We spoke of generalities for some time. When Raj Kishore had left, she looked at me and said, 'Today, you're coming with me.'

By six that evening, we were at Neelam's place. As soon as we entered, she flung her bag onto the sofa, and without making eye contact with me, said, 'You know, you're mistaken?'

I understood her meaning and said, 'How did you know what I was thinking?'

A faint, secretive smile played on her thin lips. 'Because we both thought the same thing. You perhaps gave it no further thought. But I've thought hard about it and have come to the conclusion that we were both wrong.'

'And if I say that we were both right?'

Sitting down on the sofa, she said, 'Then we're both idiots.' With this, the gravity of her expression immediately darkened. 'Sadaq, how can it be? Am I a child that I don't know what is in my heart? How old do you think I am?'

'Twenty two.'

'Exactly right. But what you don't know is that I've known about love since I was ten, and not just vicariously. God knows I've been in love. From the age of ten to sixteen, I was in the grip of a dangerous love. What effect can love have on me now?' I looked unmoved and she grew urgent: 'You're never going to believe me, are you? I could lay bare my heart to you and you still won't believe me. I know you. God help anyone who lies to you! I tell you there's no chance of my falling in love now, but I will say this much... ' Mid-sentence, she fell into silence.

I didn't say anything because she was submerged in some deep worry. She was perhaps thinking what the 'this much' she had referred to was.

After some time, that same faint, secretive smile appeared on her lips. It brought a measure of mischief to her grave expression. She suddenly jumped up from the sofa and began saying, 'I can say this much: it is not love; if it's something else, I can't say. I assure you, Sadaq... '

'You mean to say,' I said immediately, 'you assure yourself.'

She flared up. 'You really are a cretin! There are ways of saying things, you know. I mean, in the end, what need is there for me to give you assurances? Yes,

I'm trying to assure myself. The problem is that I'm not really succeeding. Aren't you going to help me?' She said this and came to sit down next to me. Clutching the little finger of her right hand, she began asking me, 'What do you think of Raj Kishore? I mean what do you think it is about Raj Kishore that I like so much?' She let go of her little finger and began clutching each of her fingers, one by one.

'I don't like his conversation, I don't like his acting, I don't like his diary, Lord knows, he talks nonsense!'

Becoming irritated, she rose. 'I can't understand what's the matter with me. But I have this urge for a bust-up, to create a commotion, for the dust to fly, and for me to be reduced to a sweating heap.' Then, turning suddenly to me, she said, 'Sadaq, what do you think, what kind of woman do you think I am?'

I smiled. 'Cats and women have always remained beyond my comprehension.'

'Why?' she shot back.

I thought about it for a moment, then answered, 'In our house, there used to be a cat. Once a year, she would succumb to bouts of mewing and crying. In answer to her cries and meows, a tomcat would appear. Then the two would brawl and fight and there would be bloodletting like you won't believe. But after it, this spinster cat would be the mother of four kittens.'

Neelam's face soured as if she had a bad taste in her mouth. 'Thooo!' she spat, 'You really are filthy.' Then after a while, sweetening her mouth with a cardamom, she said, 'I have a horror of children. But anyway, moving on.'

She opened her paan box, and with her slim fingers,

began making me a paan. With a tiny spoon, she took out the paste and powder from various silver containers, and with great care, spread them onto a deveined paan leaf. Then, folding it into a long, triangular shape, she handed it to me. 'Sadaq, what do you think?'

She said this and seemed to go blank.

'What about?' I asked.

Cutting roasted pieces of betel nut with a cutter, she replied, 'About this nonsense that has needlessly begun— if it isn't nonsense, what is it? I don't understand any of it. I feel like I'm always the one tearing everything up and forever sewing it back together. If it carries on any longer, you know what's going to happen... You have no idea, I can be a very fierce woman.'

'And what do you hope to accomplish with this fierceness?'

The same faint, hidden smile rose to Neelam's thin lips. 'You're shameless. You understand everything, but you must draw it all out, with this gentle prodding of yours.' As she said this, her eyes became bloodshot.

'Why won't you understand that I'm a very hot-tempered woman!' She rose suddenly and said, 'Now, go. I want to have a bath.'

I left.

For many days after this, Neelam said nothing about Raj Kishore to me. But we were both aware of each other's thoughts. I would know what she was thinking and she would know what I was thinking. For several days, this silent back and forth continued.

One afternoon, Kriplani, the director of *The Beauty of the Forest*, was conducting the heroine's rehearsal and we were all gathered in the music room. Neelam sat on a chair, gently keeping time with the movement of her foot. It was a popular song, but the music was good. When the rehearsal ended, Raj Kishore, his khadi bag slung over one shoulder, entered the room. He greeted director Kriplani, music director Ghosh and sound recordist PN Mogha in English, then greeted the heroine, Ms Eedan Bai, with folded hands. 'Sister Eedan, I saw you in Crawford Market yesterday. I was buying oranges for your bhabhi when I saw your car.' Swaying, talking, his gaze fell on Neelam, who sat slouched in a low chair near the piano. Immediately, he folded his hands in greeting. Neelam saw this and rose. 'Raj saab, please. Don't address me as "sister".'

She said it in a tone that, for a moment, left everyone in the music room dumbfounded. Raj Kishore flushed and managed only to say, 'Why?'

Neelam left the room without a reply.

Three days later, when I passed through Nagpara late in the afternoon, this incident was being mulled over at Sham Lal's, the paanwallah. Sham Lal was saying with great pride: 'The bitch must have a dirty mind. Otherwise, who could take offence at Raj bhai calling them "sister"? Whatever it is, she won't have her way with him. Raj bhai knows to keep his dick in his trousers.'

I was pretty fed up with Raj bhai's trousers, but I didn't say anything to Sham Lal. I sat in silence, listening to his and his client-friends' banter, in which there was mostly rumour and little truth.

The incident in the music room became known to everyone in the studio. And for three days, it was the only subject of conversation; why had Ms Neelam stopped Raj

Kishore from calling her 'sister'? I hadn't heard anything directly from Raj Kishore on the subject, but I found out through a friend of his that he'd written a riveting reflection on it in his diary, in which he'd prayed that Ms Neelam's heart and mind be cleansed of corruption.

Days passed after this incident and nothing worthy of mention occurred.

Neelam became more serious than before and Raj Kishore's kurta buttons were now always open, his pale chest bulging, its black hair poking out.

Since the rain had subsided and *The Beauty of the Forest*'s fourth set had dried, director Kriplani pasted a shooting schedule on the notice board. The scene that was to be shot was between Raj Kishore and Neelam. Because I'd written the dialogue for it, I knew that Raj Kishore, mid-conversation, was to take Neelam's hand and kiss it.

The scene didn't in any way lend itself to the kiss. But just as women are often made to wear racy clothes on screen to tantalise the audience, the director thought he'd use an old formula and add this little 'touch' of the hand kiss.

I was present on the set, my heart racing as the shooting began. What would Raj Kishore and Neelam's reaction be? Just thinking of it sent a wave of excitement through my body. But the scene was completed without incident. After every dialogue, the electric lamps, with wearying tedium, brightened and darkened. The orders to 'start' and 'cut' rang out. In the evening, when the time for the scene's climax approached, Raj Kishore played his part with great romantic flair, taking Neelam's hand in his. But just as he was about to kiss it, he turned his back to the camera, kissing his own hand and letting go of hers.

I thought Neelam would pull her hand away and slap Raj Kishore across the face, so hard that in the recording room, PN Mogha's eardrums would burst. But instead, I saw a faint smile appear on her thin lips. There wasn't a trace of a woman's hurt feelings in that smile. It was not at all what I expected of Neelam, but I didn't mention it to her. Two or three days went by without her mentioning it either, and I came to the conclusion that she had not felt the sting of the incident. Perhaps the thought had not entered her usually sensitive mind. And the only possible reason for this was that in Raj Kishore's voice, so used to referring to women as 'sister', she had been hearing terms of endearment.

Why had Raj Kishore kissed his own hand instead of Neelam's? Had he been taking revenge? Had he been trying to humiliate her? Questions arose in my mind, but no answer was forthcoming.

Four days later, when I paid my customary visit to Sham Lal's in Nagpara, he complained bitterly, 'Manto saab, you don't give us any news of what goes on in your company! You either don't want to tell us or else you don't know? Do you know what Raj bhai did?'

He recounted his own version of the story: 'There was a scene in *The Beauty of the Forest*, for which the director asked Raj bhai to kiss Ms Neelam on the mouth, but saab, can you imagine, Raj bhai on one hand, and that cheap slut on the other? Raj bhai said right away, "No, sir. This, I'm never going to do. I have a wife. Am I to return home and touch my lips to hers after I've kissed this debased woman?" That was enough, the director immediately changed the scene and said, "Alright, don't kiss her mouth, just her hand will do." But Raj saab was no amateur. When the time came, he clearly kissed his own hand, but in such a way that his audience felt he kissed this bitch's hand.'

I didn't mention any of this talk to Neelam; I felt that as she knew nothing of this entire episode, there was no point in needlessly upsetting her.

Malaria is common in Bombay. I don't remember what month it was, or the date; I only remember that the fifth set of *The Beauty of the Forest* was up and it was raining hard when Neelam suddenly succumbed to a high fever. I didn't have much work at the studio and so I sat for hours at her bedside, tending to her. The malaria had brought an unnatural yellow tone to her dark complexion. There was now a trace of helplessness in the bitter downturn of her eyes and mouth.

The quinine injections had reduced her power of hearing and she was forced to raise her frail voice when she spoke. Her own feeling was that it was me who had gone deaf.

One day, after her fever had subsided, she lay in bed, thanking Eedan Bai in a weakened voice for coming to see her, when there was the sound of a car horn downstairs. I looked; the noise sent a shudder through Neelam's body.

After a while, the room's heavy teak door opened and Raj Kishore appeared in a white kurta and close-fitting pyjamas. He entered the room with his dowdy wife at his side.

He greeted Eedan Bai as 'sister Eedan', shook my hand, and after introducing us all to his homely, tired-faced wife, sat down at Neelam's bedside. For some time, he just sat there, smiling into the emptiness. Then he turned towards Neelam, and for the first time, I saw in his clear eyes a murky emotion.

I had barely registered my surprise when he began saying in a playful tone, 'I'd been meaning to come and see you for many days, but my wretched car engine's been giving trouble. It's been lying in the workshop for the past ten days. It returned today and so I said [he gestured to his wife], "Come on Shanti, we'll go this minute. Do the housework another time. And by pure chance, today is Raksha Bandhan, we'll go and check up on sister Neelam as well as get her to tie my rakhi." '

With this, he took out a silk, tasselled rakhi from the pocket of his kurta. Neelam's sallow face became still paler, and still more distressing.

Raj Kishore didn't look in her direction. Addressing Eedan Bai, he said, 'But not like this. This is a happy occasion; my sister can't tie a rakhi on me in this state. Come on Shanti, get up. Help her put on some lipstick or something. Where is the makeup box?'

Neelam's makeup case lay on the mantelpiece. Taking two long strides, Raj Kishore brought it over. Neelam was silent. Her thin lips were tightly compressed, as if holding back a scream.

Shanti rose like an obedient wife and began putting makeup on Neelam, who offered no resistance; Eedan Bai propped up the lifeless corpse. When Shanti started painting Neelam's lips in a singularly artless fashion, she looked at me and smiled; a smile that was really a scream.

I thought, no! Any minute now, Neelam's tightly compressed lips will suddenly open, and like a mountain stream in the rains, tearing through solid dams, running madly forward, her bottled up emotions will burst forth with torrential speed, uproot us all from where we stand, and sweep us away to Lord knows what unknown depth. But to my great surprise, she didn't say a word. The yellow of her skin was concealed by the dust of rouge; and she remained as expressionless as a stone figurine. When at last she was made up, she said in a firm voice to Raj Kishore: 'Come, give it to me. I'll tie the rakhi now.'

A moment later, the silk, tasselled rakhi was on Raj Kishore's wrist. Neelam's hands, far from trembling, were tying its knot, with stony composure. As it was happening, I saw once again, in Raj Kishore's clear eyes, that same clouded emotion, but it melted into the sound of his laughter. In accordance with custom, he took out some money from an envelope and handed it to Neelam, who thanked him and put it under her pillow.

When everyone had gone, and Neelam and I were alone, she looked at me with a discomfited gaze. Then she rested her head on the pillow and remained silent. Raj Kishore had forgotten his bag on her bed. Neelam saw it and kicked it to one side. I sat for about two hours by her bedside, reading the newspaper. When she'd said nothing for a while, I got up and left without a word.

Three days after this incident, I was in my tiny, nine rupees a month room in Nagpara, shaving and listening to my neighbour, Mrs Fernandez, swear in the next door room, when I heard someone come in. I turned to look; it was Neelam.

For a moment, I thought I was mistaken; it had to be somebody else. Her dark red lipstick was smudged, making it appear as if her lips were bleeding; not a strand of hair was in place. The flowers on her white sari looked windswept. Three or four of her blouse's hooks were open and there were scratches visible on her dark breasts.

I was too shocked to see Neelam in this state to ask what had happened, or even how she'd found out where I lived.

I shut the door immediately and pulled up a chair to sit next to her. She said, 'I came straight here.'

'From where?' I asked softly.

'From my house. And I've come to say that all the bullshit is over.'

'Which?'

'I knew he'd come back to my place when there was no one there. And he did. To get his bag!' As she said this, that same faint, secretive smile played on the mouth which the lipstick had so completely defaced. 'He came to get his bag. I said, "Sure, go ahead, it's lying in the other room." There must have been something different about my tone because he looked a little frightened. I said, "Don't be afraid." But when we went into the other room, instead of giving him the bag, I sat down at the dressing table and did my makeup.'

Neelam fell silent. She picked up the glass of water on the broken table in front of us, and drank it in a few short gulps. Wiping her lips with the end of her sari, she resumed her story: 'For an hour, I did my makeup. I piled on as much lipstick as I could. I daubed my cheeks with as much rouge as they could take. He stood in silence in one corner, watching me in the mirror as I transformed into a proper witch. Then I walked with firm steps towards the door and locked it.'

'What happened then?'

I looked at Neelam for the answer to my question. She had completely changed. She had wiped her mouth with her sari, and her lips had lost all colour. The tone of her voice was subdued, like red hot iron that had been beaten down with a hammer and anvil. She didn't look like one now, but I can imagine she must truly have looked like a witch with her full makeup on.

She didn't reply immediately to my question, but rose from the charpoy and went to sit at my desk. 'I tore at him,' she said at last. 'I clung to him like a junglee cat. He clawed at my face; I clawed at his. For a long time, we wrestled with each other. And... he had the strength of a wild cat, but... But, like I once told you, I'm a fierce woman. My weakness, the weakness that the malaria had left—I didn't feel at all. My body was burning up; sparks flew from my eyes; my bones stiffened. I caught him and began fighting him like a cat. I don't know why or for what reason, I attacked him. Nothing passed between us that could be misconstrued. I was shrieking; he was groaning. I clawed the flowers from his white khadi kurta; he ripped several clumps of my hair from their root. He used all his strength, but I had already decided that victory would be mine. In the end, he lay on the carpet lifeless. I was panting, as if my breathing was about to stop. And though I was short of breath, I shredded his kurta to pieces. It was at that exact moment when I saw his firm, wide chest that I understood what it had been—what we'd tried, and failed, to understand...' She got up quickly and threw her dishevelled hair to one side with a jerk of the head. 'Sadaq,' she said, 'the bastard! His body really was beautiful. I don't know what got into me. I lowered my head and began biting into it. He just lay there, whimpering. And when I joined my bleeding mouth to his and gave him a wild, heated kiss, he became cold, like a woman resigned to her fate. I got up and felt an immediate loathing for him. I looked down at him. My blood and lipstick had left vile, almost floral bruises on his beautiful body. When I looked up at my room, everything in it seemed illusory. And so I threw open the door, from fear that I would suffocate, and came directly to you.'

With this, she was silent, like a corpse. I became afraid; I touched her hand; it hung limply at her side, and was burning hot.

'Neelam... Neelam.'

I called her name many times, but she didn't respond. When at last I called it loudly, and in a frightened voice, she gave a start. Rising to leave, she said only this: 'Saadat, my name is Radha.'

Ram Khilavan

I had just killed a bedbug, and was going through some old papers in a trunk, when I discovered Saeed bhaijan's picture. I put the picture in an empty frame lying on the table and sat down to wait for the dhobi.

Every Sunday I would wait like this, because by the end of the week, my supply of clean clothes had run out. I can hardly call it supply; in those days of poverty, I had just about enough clothes to meet my own basic standards for five or six days. My marriage was being negotiated at the time and because of this I had been going for the past two or three Sundays to Mahim.

The dhobi was an honest man. Despite my sometimes being unable to pay him, he would return my clothes every Sunday by ten. I was worried that one of these days he would grow tired of my unpaid bills and sell my clothes in the flea market, leaving me with no clothes in which to negotiate my marriage. Which, needless to say, would have been cause for great humiliation.

The vile, unmistakable stench of dead bedbugs filled my room. I was wondering how to dispel it when the dhobi arrived. With a 'salaam saab', he opened his bundle and put my clean clothes on the table. As he was doing this, his gaze fell on Saeed bhaijan's photograph. Taken aback, he looked closely at the picture and emitted a strange sound from his throat: 'He, he, he, hein?'

'What's the matter, dhobi?' I asked.

The dhobi's gaze fixed on the picture. 'But this, this is barrister Saeed Salim!'

'You know him?'

The dhobi nodded his head vigorously. 'Yes, two brothers. Lived in Colaba. Saeed Salim, barrister. I used to wash his clothes.'

Saeed Hassan bhaijan and Mahmood Hassan bhai-jan, before immigrating to Fiji, did in fact have a practice in Bombay for a year, but this would have been a few years ago.

I said, 'You're referring to a couple of years ago?'

The dhobi nodded vigorously again. 'Saeed Salim barrister when he left, he gave me one turban, one dhoti, one kurta. New. They were very nice people. One had a beard, this big.' He made a gesture with his hand to show the length of the beard. Then pointing to Saeed bhaijan's picture, said, 'He was younger. He had three little runts… they used to like to play with me. They had a house in Colaba; a big house!'

I said, 'Dhobi, they're my brothers.'

The dhobi made that strange 'he, he, he, hein?' sound again. 'Saeed Salim, barrister?'

To lessen his surprise, I said, 'This is Saeed Hassan's picture and the one with the beard is Mahmood Hassan, the eldest.'

The dhobi stared wide-eyed at me, then surveyed the squalor of my room. It was a tiny room, destitute of even an electric light. There was one table, one chair and one sack-covered cot with a thousand bedbugs. He couldn't believe I was barrister Saeed Salim's brother, but when I told him many stories about him, he shook his head incredulously and said, 'Saeed Salim, barrister lived in Colaba, and you in this quarter?'

I responded philosophically: 'The world has many colours, dhobi. Sun in places; shade in others. Five fingers are not alike.'

'Yes, saab. That is true.'

With this, he lifted his bundle and headed to the door. I remembered his bill. I had eight annas in my pocket, which would barely get me to Mahim and back. But just so that he knew I was not entirely without principles, I said, 'Dhobi, I hope you're keeping accounts. God knows how many washes I owe you for.'

The dhobi straightened the folds of his dhoti and said, 'Saab, I don't keep accounts. I worked for Saeed Salim barrister for one year. Whatever he gave me, I took. I don't know how to keep accounts.'

With this he was gone, leaving me to get dressed to go to Mahim.

The talks were successful. I got married. My finances improved too. I moved from the single room in Second Pir Khan Estates where I paid nine rupees a month, to a flat on Clear Road where I could afford to pay thirty five rupees a month. The dhobi also began to receive his payments on time.

He was pleased that my finances had improved. He said to my wife, 'Begum saab, saab's brother Saeed Salim barrister was a very big man. He lived in Colaba. When he left, he gave me a turban, one kurta and one dhoti. Your saab will also be a big man one day.'

I had told my wife the story of the picture and of the generosity the dhobi had shown me in my days of penury. When I could pay him, I had paid him, but he never complained once. But soon my wife began to complain that he never kept accounts. 'He's been working for me four years,' I told her, 'he's never kept accounts.'

She replied, 'Why would he keep accounts? That way he could take double and quadruple the amount of money.'

'How's that?'

'You have no idea. In a bachelor's household where there are no wives, there are always people who know how to make idiots of their employer.'

Nearly every month there was a dispute between my wife and the dhobi over how he did not keep an account of the clothes washed. The poor dhobi responded with complete innocence. He said, 'Begum saab, I don't know accounts, but I know you wouldn't lie. Saeed Salim barrister, who is your saab's brother, I worked for one year in his house. His begum saab would say, "Dhobi, here is your money", and I would say, "Alright."'

One month, a hundred and fifty pieces of clothing went to the wash. To test the dhobi, my wife said, 'Dhobi, this month sixty items of clothing were washed.'

He said, 'Alright Begum saab, you wouldn't lie.' When my wife paid him for sixty clothes items, he touched the money to his forehead and headed out. My wife stopped him. 'Dhobi, wait, there weren't sixty pieces of clothing, there were a hundred and fifty. Here's the rest of your money; I was just joking.'

The dhobi only said, 'Begum saab, you wouldn't lie.' He touched the rest of the money to his forehead, said 'salaam', and walked out.

Two years after I got married, I moved to Delhi. I stayed there for a year and a half before returning to Bombay, where I rented a flat in Mahim. In the span of three months, we changed dhobis four times because they were quarrelsome and crooked. After every wash, there would be a scene. Sometimes the quality of the wash was intolerably wretched; other times, too few clothes were returned. We missed our old dhobi. One day when we had gone through all our dhobis, he showed up with no warning, saying, 'I saw saab in the bus. I said, "How's this?" I made enquiries in Byculla and the brander told me to inquire here in Mahim. In the next door flat, I found saab's friend and so here I am.' We were thrilled, and at least on the laundry front, a period of joy and contentment began.

A Congress government came to power and a prohibition on alcohol was imposed. English alcohol was still available, but the making and selling of Indian alcohol was completely stopped. Ninety nine percent of the dhobis were alcoholics. That quart or half quart of alcohol, after a day spent among soap and water, was a ritual in their lives. Our dhobi had fallen ill, then tried treating his illness with the spurious alcohol that was being made illegally and sold in secret. It made him dangerously ill, bringing him close to death.

I was incredibly busy at the time, leaving the house at six in the morning and returning at ten, ten thirty at night. But when my wife heard that the dhobi was seriously ill, she went directly to his house. With the help of a servant and the taxi driver, she put him in a taxi and took him to a doctor. The doctor, moved himself by the dhobi's condition, refused money for his treatment. But my wife said, 'Doctor saab, you cannot keep all the merit of this good deed for yourself.'

The doctor smiled and said, 'Fine, let's go halves,' taking only half the money for the treatment.

In time, the dhobi was cured. A few injections got rid of his stomach infection and, with strong medicine, his weakness gradually went away. In a few months, he was completely well and sent up prayers for us every time he rose or sat down: 'May God make saab like Saeed Salim barrister; may saab be able to live in Colaba; may God give him a little brood; lots and lots of money. Begum saab came to get the dhobi in a motor car; she took him to a very big doctor near the fort; may God keep Begum saab happy.'

Many years passed. The country saw many upheavals. The dhobi came and went without fail every Sunday. He was now perfectly healthy; he never forgot what we had done for him; he still sent up prayers for us. He had also given up liquor. In the beginning, he missed it, but now he didn't so much as mention it. Despite an entire day spent in water, he felt no need for liquor to relieve his fatigue.

Then troubled times came; no sooner had Partition happened than Hindu–Muslim riots broke out. In daylight, and at night, Muslims in Hindu neighbourhoods, and Hindus in Muslim neighbourhoods, were being killed. My wife left for Lahore.

When the situation worsened, I said to the dhobi, 'Listen dhobi, you better stop your work now. This is a Muslim neighbourhood. You don't want to end up dead.'

The dhobi smiled, 'Saab, nobody will hurt me.'

There were many incidents of violence in our own neighbourhood, but the dhobi continued to come without fail.

One Sunday morning, I was at home reading the paper. The sports page showed the tally of cricket scores while the front page, that of Hindus and Muslims killed in the riots. I was focusing on the terrifying similarity of both scores when the dhobi arrived. I opened the copybook and checked the clothes against it. The dhobi started laughing and chatting. 'Saeed Salim barrister was a very nice man. When he left, he gave me one turban, one dhoti and one kurta. Your begum saab was also a first rate person. She's gone away, no? To her country? If you write her a letter, send my "salaam". She came in a motor car to my room. I had such diarrhoea. The doctor gave me an injection. I got well immediately. If you write her a letter, send my "salaam". Tell her Ram Khilavan says to write him a letter too.'

I cut him off sharply. 'Dhobi, have you started drinking again?'

He laughed, 'Drink? Where can one get drink?'

I didn't think it apposite to say more. He wrapped the dirty clothes in a bundle and went off.

In a few days, the situation became still worse. Wire after wire began to come from Lahore: 'Leave everything and come at once.' I decided at the beginning of the week that I would leave on Sunday, but as it turned out, I had to prepare to leave early the following day.

But the clothes were with the dhobi. I thought I might retrieve them from his place before the curfew started. So that evening I took a Victoria and went to Mahalakshmi.

There was an hour left before the curfew and there was still traffic on the streets, trams were still running.

My Victoria had just reached the bridge when, all of a sudden, a great commotion broke out. People ran blindly in all directions. It was as if a bullfight had begun. When the crowd thinned, I saw many dhobis in the distance with lathis in hand, dancing. Strange, indistinct sounds rose from their throats. It was where I was headed, but when I told the Victoria driver, he refused to take me. I paid him his fare and continued on foot. When I came near the dhobis, they saw me and fell silent.

I approached one dhobi and said, 'Where does Ram Khilavan live?' Another dhobi with a lathi in his hand reeled towards us. 'What's he asking?' he said to the dhobi I'd put the question to.

'He wants to know where Ram Khilavan lives.'

The blind-drunk dhobi came close to me and pushed up against me. 'Who are you?'

'Me? Ram Khilavan is my dhobi.'

'Ram Khilavan is your dhobi. But which dhobi's runt are you?'

One yelled, 'A Hindu dhobi's or a Muslim dhobi's?'

The crowd of dhobis, senselessly drunk, closed in around me with their fists up, swinging their lathis. I had to answer their question: was I Muslim or Hindu? I was terrified. The question of running away didn't arise because they had surrounded me. There were no policemen nearby to whom I could cry out for help. Dazed with fear, I started speaking in broken sentences. 'Ram Khilavan is a Hindu... I'm asking where he lives... Where is his room... He's been my dhobi for ten years... He was very sick... I had him treated... My begum... My memsaab came with a motor car... ' I got so far and felt terrible pity for myself. I was filled with shame at the depths to which men were willing to sink in order to save their lives. My wretchedness made me reckless. 'I'm Muslim,' I said.

Loud cries of 'Kill him, kill him,' rose from the crowd.

The dhobi, who was soused to the eyeballs drifted to one side, and said, 'Wait. Ram Khilavan will kill him.'

I turned and looked up. Ram Khilavan stood over me, wielding a heavy cudgel in his hand. He looked in my direction and began to hurl insults at Muslims in his language. Raising the cudgel over his head, he advanced on me, swearing the whole time.

'Ram Khilavan!' I yelled authoritatively.

'Shut your mouth!' he barked, '"Ram Khilavan …"'

My last hope had gone out. When he was close to me, I said softly, in a parched voice, 'You don't recognise me, Ram Khilavan?'

Ram Khilavan raised his cudgel in attack. Then his eyes narrowed, widened, and narrowed again. The cudgel fell from his hand. He came closer, concentrating his gaze on me and cried, 'Saab!'

He turned quickly to his companions and said, 'This is not a Muslim. This is my saab. Begum saab's saab. She came with a motor car and took me to the doctor who cured my diarrhoea.'

Ram Khilavan tried to make them understand, but they wouldn't listen. They were all drunk. Fingers were pointed this way and that. Some dhobis came over to Ram Khilavan's side and fighting broke out amongst them. I saw my chance and slipped away.

At nine the next morning my things were ready. I waited only for my ticket, which a friend had gone to buy on the black market.

I was deeply unsettled. I wanted the ticket to arrive quickly so that I could go to the port. I felt that if there were any delay, my very flat would make me a prisoner.

There was a knock on the door. I thought the ticket had arrived. I opened the door and found the dhobi standing outside.

'Salaam saab!'

'Salaam!'

'Can I come in?'

'Come in.'

He came in, in silence. He opened his bundle and put the clothes on the bed. He wiped his eyes with his dhoti, and in a choking voice, said, 'You're leaving, saab?'

'Yes.'

He began to cry. 'Saab, please forgive me. It's all the drink's fault… and… and these days it's available for free. The businessmen distribute it and say, "Drink and kill Muslims." Who's going to refuse free liquor? Please forgive me. I was drunk. Saeed Salim barrister was grateful to me. He gave me one turban, one dhoti, one kurta. Begum saab saved my life. I would have died of dysentery. She came with a motor car. She took me to the doctor. She spent so much money. You're going to the new country. Please don't tell Begum saab that Ram Khilavan…'

His voice was lost in his throat. He swung his bundle over his shoulder and headed out. I stopped him. 'Ram Khilavan, wait…'

But he straightened the folds of his dhoti and hurried out.

Licence

Abu the coachman was very stylish and his coach was number one in the city. He only took regulars. He earned ten to fifteen rupees daily from them, and it was enough for him. Unlike the other coachmen, he didn't have a taste for alcohol but he had a weakness for fashion.

Whenever his coach passed by, its bells jingling, all eyes turned to him. 'There goes that stylish Abu. Just look at the way he's sitting. And that turban, tipped to the side like that!'

When Abu heard these words and observed the admiration in people's eyes, he'd cock his head and his horse Chinni's stride would quicken. Abu held the reins as though it were hardly necessary to hold them at all, as if Chinni didn't need its master's instructions, and would keep his stride without them. At times, it seemed as though Abu and Chinni were one, or rather that the entire coach was a single life force, and who was that force, if not Abu?

The passengers Abu didn't accept cursed him roundly. Some wished him ill: 'May the Lord break his arrogance and his coach and horse land in some river.'

In the shadows cast by Abu's thin moustache, a smile of supreme self-confidence danced. It made the other coachmen burn with envy. The sight of Abu inspired them to beg, borrow and steal so that they, too, could have coaches decorated with brass fittings. But they could not replicate his distinct style and elegance. Nor did they find such devoted clients.

One afternoon, Abu was lying in his coach under the shade of a tree, dropping off to sleep, when a voice rang in his ears. Abu opened his eyes and saw a woman standing below. Abu must have looked only once at her, but her extreme youth instantly pierced his heart. She wasn't a woman, she was a girl—sixteen or seventeen; slim, but sturdy and her skin dark, but radiant. She wore silver hoops in her ears. Her hair was parted in the middle and she had a pointed nose on whose summit there was a small, bright beauty spot. She wore a long kurta, a blue skirt and a light shawl over her head.

The girl said in a childish voice, 'How much will you take for the teshan?'

Mischief played on Abu's smiling lips. 'Nothing.'

The girl's dark face reddened. 'What will you take for the teshan?' she repeated.

Abu let his eyes linger on her and replied, 'What can I take from you, fortunate one? Go on, get in the back.'

The girl covered her firm, already well concealed breasts, with her trembling hands. 'What things you say!'

Abu smiled. 'Go on, get in then. I'll take whatever you give me.'

The girl thought for a moment, then stepped onto the footboard and climbed in. 'Quickly. Come on then. Take me to the teshan.'

Abu turned around. 'In a big hurry, gorgeous?'

'You... you... ' The girl was about to say more, but stopped mid-sentence.

The carriage began to move, and kept moving; many streets passed below the horse's hooves. The girl sat nervously in the back. A mischievous smile danced on Abu's lips. When a considerable amount of time had passed, the girl asked in a frightened voice, 'The teshan hasn't come yet?'

Abu replied meaningfully, 'It'll come. Yours and my teshan is the same.'

'What do you mean?'

Abu turned to look at her and said, 'You're not such an innocent, surely? Yours and my teshan really is the same. It became one the moment Abu first set eyes on you. I swear on your life, I'm your slave; I wouldn't lie.'

The girl adjusted the shawl on her head. Her eyes showed that she understood Abu's meaning. Her face also showed that she hadn't taken his words badly. But she was mulling over this dilemma: Abu and her station might well be the same; Abu was certainly smart and dressed sharp, but was he faithful too? Should she abandon her station from which, in any case, her train had long departed, for his?

Abu's voice made her start. 'What are you thinking about, fortunate one?'

The horse was prancing along happily; the air was cold; the trees lining the street raced by; their branches swooned; there was no sound except the ringing of bells. Abu, head cocked, was fantasising about kissing the dark beauty. After some time, he tied the horse's reins to the dashboard and with a jump, landed in the back seat next to the girl. She remained silent. Abu grabbed her hands in his. 'Put your reins in my hands!'

The girl said only two words. 'Enough now.' But Abu immediately put his arms around her. She resisted. Her heart was beating hard and fast, as if it wanted to leave her and fly away.

81

'I love this horse and carriage more than life,' Abu said in a soft, loving voice, 'but I swear on the eleventh pir, I'll sell it and have gold bangles made for you. I'll wear old, torn clothes myself, but I'll keep you like a princess! I swear on the one, omnipresent God that this is the first love of my life. If you're not mine, I'll cut my throat this minute in front of you!' Then suddenly, he moved away from the girl. 'I don't know what's the matter with me today. Come on, I'll drop you to the teshan.'

'No,' the girl said softly, 'now you've touched me.'

Abu lowered his head. 'I'm sorry. I made a mistake.'

'And will you honour this mistake?'

There was a challenge in her voice, as if someone had said to Abu, 'Let's see if your carriage can go faster than mine.' He raised his lowered head; his eyes brightened. 'Fortunate one...' With this, he put his hand on his firm chest and said, 'Abu will give his life.'

The girl put forward her hand. 'Then take my hand.'

Abu held her hand firmly. 'I swear on my youth. Abu is your slave.'

The next day Abu and the girl were married. She was from Gujarat district, the daughter of a cobbler; her name was Nesti. She had come to town with her relatives. They had been waiting at the station even as Abu and she were falling in love.

They were both very happy. Abu didn't sell his horse and carriage to have gold bangles made for Nesti, but he did spend his savings on gold earrings and silk clothes for her.

His heart danced when Nesti appeared before him, her silk skirt swishing from side to side. 'I swear on the five pure ones, there's no one in the world beautiful like you are.' With this, he would press her against his chest. 'You're the queen of my heart.'

The two were immersed in the pleasures of youth. They sang; they laughed; they went on walks; they swore fidelity to each other. A month passed like this when suddenly one morning the police arrested Abu. A kidnapping case was registered against him. Nesti stood by him firmly, unwaveringly protesting his innocence, but despite that, Abu was sentenced to two years' imprisonment. When the court gave its verdict, Nesti wrapped her arms around Abu. 'I'll never go to my mother and father,' she said as she wept. 'I'll sit at home and wait for you.'

Abu gently touched her stomach. 'Bless you. I've given the horse and carriage to Dino. Carry on taking the rent from him.'

Nesti's parents put great pressure on her, but she didn't go back to them. Tiring at last, they gave up on her and left her to her lot. Nesti began to live alone. Dino would give her five rupees in the evening, which was enough for her expenses. She also received the money that had accumulated during the court case.

Abu and Nesti met once a week at the jail, meetings which were always too brief for them. Whatever money Nesti saved, she spent on bringing Abu comfort in jail. At one meeting, Abu, looking at her bare ears, asked, 'Where are your earrings, Nesti?'

Nesti smiled, and looking at the sentry, said, 'I must have lost them somewhere.'

'You needn't take so much care of me,' Abu said with some anger, 'I'm alright, however I am.'

Nesti said nothing. Their time was up. She left smiling, but when she reached home, she wept bitterly; she wept for hours because Abu's health was declining. In this last meeting, she could hardly recognise him. The strapping Abu was a shadow of his former self. Nesti thought his sorrow had consumed him and that their separation had caused his decline. What she didn't know was that Abu had TB and that the disease ran in his family. Abu's father had been even sturdier than Abu, but TB soon sent him to his grave. Abu's elder brother had also been a strapping young man, but the disease had caused him to wither away in the flower of his youth. Abu himself was unaware of this, and taking his last breath in the prison hospital, he said to Nesti in a sorrowful voice: 'If I had known I was going to die so young, I swear on the one, omnipresent God, I wouldn't have made you my wife. I've done you a great injustice. Forgive me. And listen, my horse and carriage are my hallmark. Take care of them. Stroke Chinni on the head and tell him that Abu sends his love.'

Abu died, leaving Nesti's world desolate. But she was not a woman to be easily defeated. She withstood her sorrow. The house was deserted now. In the evenings, Dino would come and comfort her. 'Have no fear, bhabhi. No one walks ahead of God. Abu was my brother. Whatever I can do for you, with God's will, I will do.'

At first Nesti didn't understand, but when her mourning period was over, Dino said in no unclear terms that she should marry him. She wanted to kick him out of the house when she heard this, but only said, 'Dino, I don't want to remarry.'

From this day on, there was a difference in the rupees Dino gave her. Earlier, he had given her five rupees daily without fail. But now he would sometimes give her four, sometimes three. His excuse was that business was slow. Then he began disappearing for two to three days at a time. Sometimes he said he was sick; other times he'd say some part of the carriage was broken and he couldn't take it out. He went too far one day and Nesti finally said, 'Listen, Dino, don't trouble yourself with it anymore. Just hand the coach and horse over to me.'

After much hemming and hawing, Dino was at last forced to place the horse and coach back in Nesti's custody. She, in turn, gave it to Maja, a friend of Abu's. Within a few days, he proposed marriage as well. When she turned him down, his eyes changed; the warmth in them seemed to vanish. Nesti took the horse and carriage back from him and gave it to a coachman she didn't know. He really broke all boundaries, arriving completely drunk one night to give her the money, and making a grab for her as soon as he walked through the door. She let him have it and fired him at once.

For eight or ten days, the coach was in the stable, out of work, racking up costs—feed on one hand, stable rent on the other. Nesti was in a state of confusion. People were either trying to marry her or rape her or rob her. When she went outside, she was met with ugly stares. One night a neighbour jumped the wall and started making advances towards her. Nesti went half mad wondering what she should do.

One day as she sat at home, she thought 'What if I were to drive the coach myself?' When she used to go on rides with Abu, she would often drive it herself. She was acquainted with the routes as well. But then she thought of what people would say. Her mind came up with many rejoinders. 'What's the harm? Do women not toil and do manual labour? Here working in mines, there in offices, thousands working at home; you have to fill your stomach one way or the other!'

She spent a few days thinking about it. At last she decided to do it. She was confident she could. And so, after asking God's help, she arrived one morning at the stable. When she began harnessing the horse to the carriage, the other coachmen were stupefied; some thought it was a joke and roared with laughter. The older coachmen tried dissuading her, saying it was unseemly. But Nesti wouldn't listen. She fitted up the carriage, polished its brass tackle, and after showing the horse great affection and speaking tender words to Abu, she set out from the stable. The coachmen were stunned at Nesti's dexterity; she handled the carriage expertly.

Word spread through the town that a beautiful woman was driving a coach. It was spoken of on every street corner. People waited impatiently for the moment when she would come down their street.

At first Nesti shied away from male passengers, but she soon lost her shyness and began taking in an excellent income. Her coach was never idle, here passengers got off, there they got on. Sometimes passengers would even fight among themselves over who had stopped her first.

When the work became too much, she had to fix hours for when the coach would go out—in the mornings, from seven to twelve; in the afternoons, from two to six. This arrangement proved beneficial as she managed to get enough rest as well. Chinni was happy too, but Nesti couldn't help being aware that her clients often rode in her coach only to be near her. They would make her go aimlessly from pillar to post, sometimes cracking dirty jokes in the back. They spoke to her just to hear the sound of her voice. Sometimes she felt that though she had not sold herself, people had slyly bought her anyway. She was also aware that all the city's other coachmen thought ill of her. But she was unperturbed; her belief in herself kept her at peace.

One morning, the municipal committee men called her in and revoked her licence. Their reason was that women couldn't drive coaches. Nesti asked, 'Sir, why can't women drive coaches?'

The reply came: 'They just can't. Your licence is revoked.'

Nesti said, 'Sir, then take my horse and coach as well, but please tell me why women can't drive coaches. Women can grind mills and fill their stomachs. Women can carry rubble in baskets on their heads and make a living. Women can work in mines, sifting through pieces of coal to earn their daily bread. Why can't I drive a coach? I know nothing else. The horse and carriage were my husband's, why can't I use them? How will I make ends meet? My Lord, please have mercy. Why do you stop me from hard, honest labour? What am I to do? Tell me.'

The officer replied: 'Go to the bazaar and find yourself a spot. You're sure to make more that way.'

Hearing this, the real Nesti, the person within, was reduced to ashes. 'Yes sir,' she answered softly and left. She sold the horse and carriage for whatever she could get and went straight to Abu's grave. For a moment, she stood next to it in silence. Her eyes were completely dry, like the blaze after a shower, robbing the earth of all its moisture. Her lips parted and she addressed the grave: 'Abu, your Nesti died today in the committee office.'

With this, she went away. The next day she submitted her application. She was given a licence to sell her body.

The Mice of Shah Daulah

Salima was twenty one when she was married. And though five years had passed, she had not had a child. Her mother and mother-in-law were very worried. Her mother, more so, for fear that her husband, Najib, would marry again. Many doctors were consulted, but none were of any help.

Salima was anxious too. Few girls do not desire a child after marriage. She consulted her mother and acted on her instructions, but to no avail.

One day a friend of hers came to see her. She had been declared barren and so Salima was surprised to see that she held a flower of a boy. 'Fatima,' she asked indelicately, 'how did you produce this boy?'

Fatima was five years older than Salima. She smiled and said, 'This is the benevolence of Shah Daulah. A woman told me that if I wanted children, I should go to the shrine of Shah Daulah in Gujarat and make my entreaty. Say, "Hazur, the first child born to me, I will offer up in your service."' This child would be born with a very small head, she told Salima. Salima didn't like this. And when Fatima insisted that this firstborn child had to be left in the service of the shrine, she was sadder still. She thought, what mother would deprive herself of her child forever? Only a monster could abandon its child, whether his head be small, his nose flat or his eyes crossed. But Salima wanted a child badly and so she heeded her older friend's advice.

She was, in any case, native to Gujarat where Shah Daulah's shrine was. So she said to her husband,

'Fatima's insisting I go with her. Would you give me permission?' What objection could her husband have? He said, 'Go, but come back quickly.' Salima went off with Fatima.

Shah Daulah's shrine was not, as she had thought, some old, decrepit building. It was a decent place which she liked well enough. But when in one chamber, she saw Shah Daulah's 'mice', with their running noses and their minds enfeebled, she began to tremble. There was a young girl, in the prime of her youth, whose antics were such that she could reduce the most serious of serious people to laughter. Watching her, Salima laughed to herself for an instant. Then immediately her eyes filled with tears. What will become of this girl, she thought. The shrine's caretakers will sell her to somebody who'll take her from town to town like a performing monkey; the wretch, she'll become somebody's source of income. Her head was very small. But Salima thought, even if her head is small, her heart can't be similarly small; that remains the same, even in madmen.

The Shah Daulah's mouse had a beautiful body, rounded and proportionate in every way. But her antics were those of one whose faculties had been decimated. Seeing her wander about, laughing like a wind-up doll, Salima felt as if she'd been made for this purpose.

And yet, despite her misgivings, Salima followed her friend Fatima's advice and prayed at Shah Daulah's shrine, swearing that if she had a child, she would hand him over.

Salima continued her medical treatment as well. After two months, she showed signs of pregnancy. She was thrilled. A boy was soon born to her, a beautiful boy. There had been a lunar eclipse during her pregnancy, and he was born with a small, not unattractive, mark on his right cheek.

Fatima came to visit and said that the boy should be handed over at once to Shah Daulah saab. Salima herself had accepted this, but she had been delaying it for many days; the mother in her wouldn't allow her to go through with it; she felt as though a part of her heart was being cut out.

She had been told that the firstborn of those who asked a child of Shah Daulah would have a small head. But her son's head was quite big. Fatima said, 'This is not something you can use as an excuse. This child of yours is Shah Daulah's property. You have no right over him. If you stray from your promise, remember that a scourge will befall you, the likes of which you won't forget for a lifetime.'

So, with her heart breaking, Salima went back to Gujarat, to the shrine of Shah Daulah, and handed to its caretakers, her beloved flower of a son, with the black mark on his right cheek.

She wept. Her grief was so great she became sick. For a year, she hovered between life and death. She couldn't forget her boy nor the pleasing mark on his right cheek, which she had so often kissed.

She had strange dreams. Shah Daulah, in her distressed imagination, became a large mouse gnawing, with its razor edged teeth, at her flesh. She would shriek and implore her husband to help her. 'Look, he's eating my flesh!' she would cry.

91

Sometimes her fevered mind would see her son entering a mouse hole. She would be holding onto his tail, but the bigger mice had him by the snout and she couldn't pull him out.

Sometimes the girl whom she'd seen in a chamber of Shah Daulah's shrine, the girl in the flower of her youth, would appear before her, and Salima would let out a laugh. Then a moment later, she would begin to cry. She would cry so much that her husband wouldn't know how to quell her tears.

Salima saw mice everywhere, in bed, in the kitchen, in the bathroom, on the sofa, in her heart. Sometimes she felt she herself was a mouse: her nose was running, she was in a chamber of Shah Daulah's shrine, carrying her tiny head on her weak shoulders, and her antics made onlookers fall over themselves with laughter. Her condition was pitiable.

Her world had been marked, like a face on which the fragments of a dead sun had become stuck.

The fever subsided, and Salima's condition stabilised. Najib was relieved. He knew the cause of his wife's illness, but he was in the grip of superstition himself and hardly conscious that he had offered up his firstborn as a sacrifice. Whatever had been done seemed right to him; in fact, he felt that the son that had been born to him was not even his, but Shah Daulah saab's. When Salima's fever, along with the storm in her mind and soul, cooled, Najib said to her, 'My darling, you must forget your son. He was meant for sacrifice.'

Salima replied in a wounded voice, 'I don't believe in any of it. All my life I will curse myself for committing so great a wrong and handing over a piece of my heart to those caretakers. They cannot be its mother.'

One day, Salima disappeared to Gujarat and spent eight or nine days there, making enquiries about her son, but learnt nothing of his whereabouts. She returned, depressed, and said to her husband, 'Now I won't remember him any longer.'

Remember him, she did, but deep within herself. The mark on her son's right cheek had branded itself in her heart.

A year later Salima had a daughter. Her face bore a great resemblance to her firstborn's although she didn't have a mark on her right cheek. Salima called her Mujiba because she had intended to name her son Mujib.

When she was two months old, Salima sat her in her lap, and taking a little kohl, made a large beauty spot on her right cheek. Then she thought of Mujib and wept. When her tears fell on her daughter's cheeks, she wiped them with her dupatta and laughed. She wanted to try and forget her grief.

Salima had two sons thereafter. Her husband was now very pleased. Finding herself in Gujarat for a friend's wedding, she returned again to the shrine and made enquiries about her Mujib, but to no avail. She thought that perhaps he had died. And so, one Thursday, she organised a memorial for him.

The women of the neighbourhood wondered whose death these rites were being so carefully observed for. Some even questioned Salima, but she gave no reply.

In the evening she took her ten year old Mujiba by the hand and led her inside. She made a spot on her right cheek with kohl and kissed it profusely.

She had always imagined her to be her lost Mujib, but now she gave up thinking about him. After the ceremony the weight in Salima's heart lightened. She had made a grave for him in her imagination, and still in her imagination, she would place flowers on it.

Salima's three children were now in school. Every morning she dressed them, made them breakfast, got them ready and sent them off. When they'd gone she'd think for a moment of Mujib, and the ceremony she had done for him. Her heart was lighter and yet she felt sometimes that the mark on Mujib's right cheek was still branded on it.

One day her three children came running in, saying, 'Ammi, we want to see the show.'

'What show?' she asked lovingly.

Her eldest daughter replied, 'Ammi, there's a man who does the show.'

Salima said, 'Go and call him, but not in the house. He should do the show outside.'

The children ran off, came back with the man and watched the show.

When it was over Mujiba went to her mother to ask for money. Her mother took out a quarter rupee from her purse and went out onto the veranda. She had reached the door when she saw one of Shah Daulah's mice moving his head in a crazed fashion. Salima began to laugh.

There were ten or twelve children around him, laughing uncontrollably. The noise was so great that no one could hear a word.

Salima advanced with the quarter rupee in her hand, but just as she was about to give it to Shah Daulah's mouse, her hand was flung back as though struck by an electric current.

This mouse had a mark on its right cheek. Salima looked closely at him. His nose was running. Mujiba, who was standing near him, said to her mother, 'This, this mouse, Ammi, why does he look so much like me? Am I a mouse too?'

Salima took Shah Daulah's mouse by the hand and went inside. She closed the door and kissed him and said prayers for him. He was her Mujib. But his antics were so moronic that Salima laughed even though her heart was filled with grief

She said to Mujib, 'My son, I am your mother.'

At this, the mouse laughed uproariously, and wiping his runny nose on his sleeve, stood with his hands open before his mother and said, 'One paisa!'

His mother opened her purse, but by then her eyes had begun to overflow with tears. She took out a hundred rupees from her purse and went out to give it to the man who had made a spectacle of Mujib. He refused, saying that he couldn't part with his means of income for such a small amount. In the end Salima got him to settle on five hundred rupees. But when she came back inside, Mujib was gone. Mujiba told her that he had run out of the back door.

Salima's womb cried out for him to return, but he'd gone, never to return.

For Freedom

I no longer remember the year, but they were days when 'Long Live the Revolution' rang through the streets of Amritsar. There was a youthfulness to those slogans; they seemed to have something of the spirit of the region's peasantry who, with baskets of manure on their heads, would slice through the city's bazaars. What days they were! The fear that had hung in the air after Jallianwala Bagh had wholly disappeared. And a fearless longing had taken its place, a blind abandon, ignorant of all destination.

People shouted slogans, held demonstrations, were arrested in the dozens. Getting arrested became an amusing pastime—arrested in the morning; released in the evening; tried; sentenced to a few months in prison; released; a slogan shouted; imprisoned again.

They were days full of life. A tiny bubble could burst and cause a whirlpool. Someone standing in a square might say, 'There should be a strike.' And there was a strike. A ripple would rise: every man ought to wear khadi so that all Lancashire's mills would close, and a boycott on foreign cloth would begin, pyres springing up in every square. People became impassioned, and then and there, tore off their clothes and flung them into the fire. If some woman threw down an unwanted sari from her balcony, the crowd applauded till its hands were sore.

I remember a bonfire outside a police station near the town hall. Sheikhoo, a classmate of mine, grew impassioned, and taking off his silk coat, threw it into the bonfire of foreign cloth. A sea of applause rose because Sheikhoo was the son of a well-known toady. The poor fool, growing still more passionate, took off his silk kurta and surrendered it to the fire. He only realised later that his gold buttons had gone with it!

But, I can't mock Sheikhoo; I was pretty wild in those days myself. I wanted to get my hands on a pistol and start a terrorist organisation. It didn't even occur to me that my father was a government pensioner; there was ferment in my heart akin to the kind one has in a game of flash.

School had never really interested me, but during that time, I developed a hatred for my studies. I'd leave the house with my books and head straight to Jallianwala Bagh. I'd stay there till the school day was over, observing the political activities or just lying under a tree's shadow, looking at the women in the windows of houses beyond, certain that I would soon fall in love with one of them. Why, I can't say.

There was plenty of bustle at the time in Jallianwala Bagh. Tents and makeshift walls had come up everywhere. In the biggest camp, every two or three days, a 'dictator' was appointed who all the volunteers would offer their salaams to. For two to three days, ten to fifteen at the maximum, this dictator would sit there, khadi clad, accepting the greetings of men and women with feigned seriousness. He would collect rice and wheat from the city's merchants for the communal kitchen and drink endless lassis, which always seemed to be abundant in Jallianwala Bagh. Then, suddenly one day, he'd be arrested and taken off to prison.

I had an old classmate called Shahzada Ghulam Ali. The facts I'm about to recount now will give you some idea of our friendship: we failed the matric exam together, twice; we ran away from home once and went to Bombay. We thought we'd go on to Russia, but our money ran out and we were forced to sleep on pavements, at which point, we wrote letters home, begged forgiveness and made our way back.

Shahzada Ghulam Ali was a beautiful young man. He was tall and fair in the Kashmiri way, with a fine nose, playful eyes and great, rakish charm.

When we were in school, he was not called Shahzada, but later, the city's revolutionary activities took hold of him. He attended some ten–fifteen meetings, and the demonstrations, the slogans, the garlands of marigolds, the passionate songs, the talk of freedom with lady volunteers, turned him into an amateur revolutionary. Then, one morning he made his first speech. The following day I read in the newspaper that Ghulam Ali had been made Shahzada.

Ghulam Ali became famous throughout Amritsar after he was made Shahzada. It was a small town; it didn't take long to acquire either a good reputation or a bad one. Where average men were concerned, Amritsaris were very discerning. They were forever exposing each other's failings, but turned a blind eye to those of their leaders. Perhaps because they were always hungry for a political movement or a stirring speech. A man could be white one day and black the next, but in Amritsar, by changing his colours, a politician could stay alive quite a while. It was a different time—all the big leaders were in jail, their chairs were empty, and though the people had no special need of leaders, the current movement desperately needed men willing to sit, khadi clad, for a day or two in Jallianwala Bagh's big tents before making a speech and getting arrested.

At the time, new dictatorships sprang up all across Europe. Hitler and Mussolini were being heavily promoted. And perhaps under this influence, the Congress party began churning out 'dictators' of its own. By the time it came round to Shahzada Ghulam Ali's turn, some forty 'dictators' had already been arrested.

I rushed to Jallianwala Bagh as soon as I found out that Ghulam Ali had been made dictator. Outside the big tent, there was a volunteers' guard. But when Ghulam Ali saw me from inside, he waved me in. There was a mattress on the floor, over which a khadi cover had been draped. It was on this that Ghulam, leaning against a bolster, sat with a few khadi clad merchants, discussing vegetables, I believe. In a few a minutes, he finished this conversation, gave a few volunteers their orders, and turned his attention towards me. It tickled me to see this uncharacteristic seriousness, and when he sent away the volunteers, I laughed out loud. 'So then, Mr Shahzada, tell me more?'

And though I sat there at length, poking fun at Ghulam Ali, I sensed a change in him, a change of which he was not unaware himself. He said many times to me, 'Don't Saadat, don't make fun of me. I know that the head is small and the crown big, but from now on, this is my life.'

Every evening Jallianwala Bagh filled with people. Because I came early, I found a place close to the platform.

Ghulam Ali appeared after loud applause, handsome and attractive, in spotless white khadi clothes. His rakish charm made him seem still more attractive. He spoke for about an hour. During the course of the speech, there were many moments when the hairs on my body stood on end. Once or twice, I even wished that I could explode like a bomb, thinking perhaps India might become free if I did.

The years that have passed since then! To now recount that time and the feelings it aroused in us, is difficult. But as I sit down to write this story, and think of Ghulam Ali's speech, it is the voice of youth, a youth wholly untainted by politics, that rings in my ears. It contained the pure fearlessness of a young man who seemed, in a moment, to be able to grab a young woman, also travelling the road, and to say to her, 'Listen, I want you', and in the next, to be imprisoned by the law. Since then, I've had the good fortune to listen to many more speeches, but that madness, that extreme youth, that adolescent feeling, the boyish timbre I heard that night in Shahzada Ghulam Ali's voice, I haven't heard so much as a faint echo of again. The speeches I hear now are cold, serious, heavy with stale politics and writerly glibness.

At that time, both the government as well as the public were still inexperienced. They were at each other's throats with no thought of the consequences. The government imprisoned people without understanding what it meant. And the imprisoned went to jail without knowing what their objective was.

It was a sham of sorts, but a combustible sham. People leapt up like flames, burnt and died, then flamed again. And with this flaming and dying, the sad, sleep-filled atmosphere of bondage was infused with a fiery dynamism.

When Shahzada Ghulam Ali's speech ended, all of Jallianwala Bagh was alight with applause and slogans. Ghulam Ali's face glowed with emotion. When I went up to the stage and pressed his hand in congratulation, I could feel it shaking. He seemed breathless. Besides the passion in his eyes, I thought I also saw a kind of hunger. He seemed to be searching for someone. And then suddenly, he separated his hand from mine and walked in the direction of a jasmine bush. A girl stood there, dressed in a spotless khadi sari.

The next day, I heard that Shahzada Ghulam Ali was in the grip of a new love. It was the girl I had seen standing deferentially near the jasmine bush. And his love was not unreturned; Nigar was just as captivated by him. As apparent from the name, Nigar was a Muslim girl, and an orphan. She was a nurse at the women's hospital and perhaps the first Muslim girl to step out of purdah to join the Congress' movement.

Her khadi dress, her participation in the Congress' activities and her work at the hospital had worn down Nigar's Islamic rigidity—that particular severity one finds in all Muslim girls—softening her slightly.

She was not beautiful, but a singular specimen of womanhood. The combination of humility and selflessness that characterises dutiful Hindu women, making them worthy of worship, was blended lightly into Nigar, producing a colour in her that lifted the soul. Though at the time it did not occur to me, as I write now, and think of Nigar, I feel that she was like a beguiling compound of Muslim prayer and Hindu ritual.

Nigar worshipped Shahzada Ghulam Ali and he, too, was devoted to her. When I spoke to him about her, I discovered that they had met during the Congress' movement. And within a few days of their first meeting, they had sworn love to one another.

Ghulam Ali intended to make Nigar his wife before he went to jail. I can't remember what his reasons were, as he could just as easily have married her when he returned from jail. In those days, no one went for very long: three months at the minimum and a year at the outside; some were released after no more than fifteen to twenty days so that room could be made for new prisoners. But he'd expressed this intention to Nigar and she was absolutely ready. All that was left to be done was to obtain Babaji's blessings.

Babaji, as you might know, was an important figure. At the time, he was staying a little outside the city, at the luxurious house of the millionaire Lala Hari Ram Siraf. He spent most of his time at the ashram he'd built in a nearby village, but when in Amritsar, he only stayed at Lala Hari Ram's house. With his arrival, the house became a place of pilgrimage for his followers. All day a stream of devotees flowed through it. At the end of the day, he would sit outside the house, on a raised platform under a cluster of mango trees, and meet people and receive donations for his ashram. Once he'd listened to a few minutes of devotional singing, he'd bring the audience to an end.

Babaji was a pious, compassionate, learned man and for this reason Hindus, Muslims, Sikhs and untouchables alike became his followers, considering him their spiritual leader.

He showed no interest in politics, but it was an open secret that every political movement in Punjab began and ended at his ashram.

In the eyes of the government, he was a problem with no solution, a political enigma that its mightiest intellectuals couldn't crack. A faint smile from his thin lips was interpreted in a thousand different ways. And Babaji would unveil yet another meaning, leaving a mesmerised public still more mesmerised.

The ongoing civil disobedience movement in Amritsar, which was rapidly sending people to prison, was the work of Babaji's ashram. Every evening, in his open meetings, he would issue a small statement from his toothless mouth regarding the freedom movement in Punjab and the government's draconian policies. The most important leaders would cling to his words as though they were sacred amulets.

People swore that his eyes possessed a magnetic power; that there was a kind of magic in his voice; and then the cool of that smiling mind, which the filthiest insult and the most poisonous abuse could not, for even a fraction of a moment, perturb! It was this that was the cause of so much distress to his opponents.

Babaji had held several demonstrations in Amritsar. But I, for some reason, despite having seen all the other leaders, had never laid eyes on him, not even from a distance. And so, when Ghulam Ali spoke to me of going to see him to request his permission to marry, I asked to be taken along as well. The following day, Ghulam Ali organised a horse carriage and we set out early for Lala Hari Ram luxurious house.

Babaji, having completed his ablutions and morning prayers, was listening to a beautiful panditani singing patriotic songs. He sat on a fig leaf mat spread out over a floor of sugar white tiles. A bolster lay near him, but he didn't use it for support.

Except for the mat on which Babaji sat, there was no furniture in the room. From one edge of it to the other, the white tiles gleamed. Their gleam seemed to accentuate the panditani's beauty, with her faintly onion pink cheeks and her patriotic songs.

Babaji would have been older than seventy, but his body (he only wore a saffron-coloured loincloth) was free of wrinkles. There was a glow to his skin. I later found out that every morning before bathing, he had olive oil rubbed into his body. He glanced briefly at Shahzada Ghulam Ali, then looked at me as well and, responding to our greeting with a smile, gestured to us to sit down.

Looking back, I find the scene not only interesting, but worthy of close attention. Sitting before me in an ascetic's asana on a fig leaf mat was an old, half naked man. His posture, his bald head, his half open eyes, his dark, soft body, his face's every feature, emanated resolve. He seemed to know that the mightiest earthquake could not unseat him from the pedestal on which the world had placed him. Some distance from him, a newly blossomed flower of the Kashmir valley bowed reverentially. She bowed both out of respect for being in the presence of this elderly man, and because she was moved by her own patriotic song. Her extreme youth seemed to want to break out of the rough white sari she wore, and to sing not just patriotic songs, but songs of her youth which, apart from revering this elderly man, might also have liked to honour some young, vigorous figure who'd grab her soft wrist and take her headlong into the roaring bonfire of life. A silent contest seemed to arise between the girl's onion pink cheeks, dark, lively eyes and storm-filled breasts, concealed in a rough khadi blouse, and the old ascetic's robust conviction and stony satisfaction. It seemed to say, 'Come, either unseat me from this place where I sit now and pull me down, or take me still higher.'

The three of us, Shahzada Ghulam Ali, Nigar and I, went to one side and sat down. I was struck dumb. Babaji's presence as well as the panditani's unstained beauty were very affecting. Even the floor's gleaming tiles transfixed me. I found myself thinking, even if she allows me to do nothing else, I want to kiss her eyes. The image sent a shiver through my body. My mind jumped immediately to thoughts of my maid, whom I'd recently developed something of a crush on. I felt for a moment like leaving them all there and rushing home; perhaps I'd be successful in taking her up to the bathroom without anyone seeing. But when my gaze returned to Babaji and the patriotic song's passion-filled lyrics rang in my ears, I felt a different kind of frisson go through my body. I thought, if only I could get my hands on a pistol, I'd go down to Civil Lines and make a small start by gunning down the English.

Next to me sat Nigar and Ghulam Ali, two people in love. It had been unconsummated for too long and now, perhaps a little tired, they wished for it to swiftly reveal its colours with their becoming one. And this was what they had really come to ask Babaji, their spiritual leader, permission for. In that moment, apart from the patriotic song, the beautiful, but yet unheard words of their own life song were ringing in their ears.

The song finished. Babaji blessed the panditani with great tenderness. Smiling, he turned to Nigar and Ghulam Ali, looking briefly at me as well.

Ghulam Ali was about to introduce himself, but Babaji had an excellent memory. He said immediately in his sweet voice, 'Shahzada, you haven't been arrested yet?'

Ghulam Ali folded his hands and said, 'Sir, no.'

Babaji took out a single pencil from the pen holder and began to play with it. 'But I was under the impression,' he said, 'that you had already been arrested.'

Ghulam Ali didn't understand his meaning. Babaji turned to the panditani, and pointing to Nigar, said, 'Nigar has arrested our Shahzada.'

Nigar reddened; Ghulam Ali's mouth fell open with surprise; the panditani's onion pink cheeks acquired a serene glow. She looked at Nigar and Ghulam Ali as if to say, 'This is very good news.'

Babaji once again turned towards the panditani. 'These children have come to ask my permission to marry. And what of you, Kamal? When will you marry?'

So this panditani's name was Kamal! Babaji's sudden question made her start; her onion pink complexion turned red.

In a trembling voice, she replied, 'But I am to go to your ashram.'

A faint sigh seemed wrapped up in these words, which Babaji's quick mind took instant note of. He continued to look at her, and smiling in his ascetic's way, addressed Ghulam Ali and Nigar, 'So, the two of you have made your decision?'

'Yes,' they both replied in subdued voices.

Babaji looked at them with his fine eyes. 'When men make decisions, they sometimes have to unmake them as well.'

Despite Babaji's formidable presence, Ghulam Ali's naive, fearless youth spoke. 'This decision might, for some reason, have to be altered, but it won't be unmade.'

Babaji closed his eyes, and in a lawyerly tone, asked, 'Why?'

Ghulam Ali, surprisingly, was not the slightest bit perturbed. Perhaps this time, the purity of his love for Nigar spoke. 'Babaji, take the decision we've made to free India. Now, perhaps Time will alter our plans, but the decision itself will stand.'

Babaji, I felt, didn't think it apposite to argue the point. And so, he smiled. The meaning of this smile, like all his smiles, could be interpreted in completely different ways. And if Babaji were to have been asked what it meant, I'm certain he would have drawn out yet another interpretation, entirely different from ours.

But, anyway! This many layered smile widened on his thin lips, and turning to Nigar, Babaji said, 'Nigar, you come to our ashram. Shahzada will in any case be arrested any day now.'

'Yes, alright,' she replied in a quiet voice.

After this, Babaji turned the conversation away from the subject of marriage and towards the political activities in the Jallianwala Bagh camp. Ghulam, Nigar and Kamal sat at length, discussing arrests, releases, milk, lassi and vegetables while I, still struck dumb, was left wondering why Babaji had been so tentative in giving his consent to the marriage. Did he doubt Ghulam Ali and Nigar's love for each other? Did he mistrust Ghulam Ali's integrity? Had he invited Nigar to the ashram so that she might forget her soon to be imprisoned fiancé? And as for Babaji's question, 'When will you marry, Kamal?', why had Kamal replied, 'But I am to go to your ashram'? Did men and women not marry in the ashram? My mind came under the grip of a strange turmoil even as those around me discussed whether the lady volunteers would be able to prepare chapattis on time for five hundred. Were there enough chickpeas? How big was the pan? And couldn't a single large wood stove be constructed with a pan of the same size, on which as many as six women could make rotis simultaneously?

I wondered whether Kamal, the panditani, would spend her time in the ashram singing patriotic and devotional songs for Babaji. I had met some of the ashram's male volunteers. The whole lot of them, according to the rules of the place, rose early, bathed, brushed their teeth, lived in the open, sang devotional songs, but their clothes reeked of sweat, often their breath was bad and that colour and vigour that comes to men when they live in the outdoors was entirely absent in them.

Stooped, subdued, sallow, sunken-eyed and weak-bodied, like some cow's deflated udders, lifeless and inert, yes, I'd seen the ashram's men often in Jallianwala Bagh. But now I wondered, would the murky eyes of these same men who stank somehow of stale grass ogle this panditani made of milk, honey and saffron? Would these same men, with their foul-smelling breath, make conversation with this fragranced creature? Then I checked myself, India's independence was more important than these considerations; maybe.

For all my love of my country and my passion for independence, I couldn't quite comprehend this 'maybe' because at that moment I thought of Nigar, sitting next to me, telling Babaji that turnips take a long time to soften. Where were turnips and where was the marriage that she and Ghulam Ali had come to seek permission for!

I began to think of Nigar in the ashram. I hadn't seen it myself, but I have always—I'm not sure why—felt a hatred for these places that go by the names of ashrams, shelters, seminaries and retreats. I have on many occasions seen the students and administrators of these shelters for the blind and orphaned, walking the streets in a column, begging for money. I have seen seminaries and madrasas with boys in shortened religious pyjamas, their foreheads calloused from prayer, in childhood; the older ones, with their thick, black beards; the younger, with that truly repugnant combination of thick and fine hair on their cheeks and chins. They carry on piously reading their prayers, but in each of their eyes, animal passions are clearly visible.

Nigar was a woman, not a Muslim, Hindu or Christian woman, just a woman; no, she was more than that, she was like a prayer incarnate of her love for Ghulam Ali. A woman like this had no need to raise her hands in prayer at Babaji's ashram, where daily prayer was a regulation.

When I look back now, Babaji, Nigar, Ghulam Ali, the beautiful panditani and Amritsar's entire atmosphere at that time, infused with the romance of the independence movement, appear to me like a dream, a dream which, once dreamt, begs to be dreamt again. And though I still haven't seen Babaji's ashram, the antipathy I possessed for it then, I still possess now.

I have no regard for those places where men are frogmarched along rules that run contrary to their nature. Attaining independence was, without a doubt, the right thing to do and I could understand it if a man should die in attaining it, but that some poor wretch should be defanged, made as benign as a vegetable for its sake— this was utterly beyond my comprehension.

Living in huts, forsaking bodily comforts, singing God's praises, shouting patriotic slogans—all this was fine, but to slowly deaden one's senses, one's bodily desires— what was meant by that? What was left of a man in whom the longing for beauty and drama had died? What distinctiveness, what particularity could remain then between the various pastures of these ashrams, madrasas, shelters and retreats?

Babaji sat at length, talking to Ghulam Ali and Nigar about the political activities at Jallianwala Bagh. At last, he said to this couple who, naturally, hadn't forgotten their original purpose in coming to see him, that they should come the following evening to Jallianwala Bagh, where they would be made man and wife.

Ghulam Ali and Nigar were elated. What better fortune could they have than Babaji himself conducting their marriage ceremony. Ghulam Ali told me much later, that he was so happy at the news that he felt he had misheard it. Even a slight gesture from Babaji's frail hands became a historical incident. Would such a great personage really come to Jallianwala Bagh to take interest in the marriage of an ordinary man such as himself, who had only by accident become the Congress 'dictator'! Surely, it would be front page news in every newspaper in India.

Ghulam Ali was sure that Babaji wouldn't come; he would be too busy—although he said this in the hope that the opposite would occur. He was proved wrong. At six in the evening in Jallianwala Bagh, when bushes of raat ki rani prepared to diffuse their fragrance, and countless volunteers, after erecting a tent for the bride and groom, now decorated it with jasmine and roses, Babaji, accompanied by the patriotic, song-singing panditani, his secretary and Lala Hari Ram, arrived, pawing the ground with his stick. News of his arrival reached Jallianwala Bagh the moment Lala Hari Ram's green car stopped in front of the main entrance.

I was there too. In one tent, the lady volunteers were dressing Nigar up as a bride. Ghulam Ali had made no special preparations. He had spent most of the day with the city's Congress merchants, discussing the volunteers' needs. His few spare moments, he spent talking to Nigar in private. He didn't brief his subordinate officers any more than telling them that Nigar and he wished to raise the flag after the marriage ceremony.

When Ghulam Ali received news of Babaji's arrival, he was standing near the well. I was perhaps telling him at the time: 'Ghulam Ali, do you know that when the bullets flew here, this well became full to the brim with bodies. Today, everyone drinks its water. The garden's flowers soak it up and people come and pick the flowers. And yet, there's never the salty taste of blood in the water or flower buds carrying something of its redness. What a thing!'

I remember well, I said this and looked ahead at the window of a house from which it is said that a young girl had sat watching the scenes below, when she became the victim of one of General Dyer's stray bullets. The streaks of blood from her chest faded slowly from the house's old walls.

But blood had become cheap, and spilling it hardly produced the same effect anymore. I remember that seven or eight months after the massacre in Jallianwala Bagh, my third or fourth grade teacher had brought the entire class here. The garden then was not a garden; it was a dry, desolate, uneven piece of land where, at every step, one's foot knocked against the lumpy earth. I remember our teacher finding a piece of mud, stained perhaps with paan spittle. 'Look,' he said, holding it up before the class, 'it's still stained with the blood of our martyrs.'

As I write this story, countless other incidents, etched into my memory, rise to the surface. But yes, I was recounting the story of Ghulam Ali and Nigar's wedding!

When Ghulam Ali heard of Babaji's arrival, he rushed to gather all the other volunteers, who greeted Babaji with a military style salute. After this, he and Ghulam Ali spent considerable time doing the rounds of the various camps. Babaji, who had a sharp sense of humour, cracked a number of one-liners as he spoke to the lady volunteers and other workers.

When candles could be seen burning in the occasional window, and a kind of half-light fell over Jallianwala

Bagh, all the female volunteers began to sing devotional songs in one voice. A few were harmonious; the rest, tuneless. But their collective effect was pleasing. Babaji closed his eyes and listened. About one thousand people were present, sitting around the stage on the floor. Except for the girls singing devotional songs, everybody else sat in silence.

The singing ended and for some moments a pregnant silence prevailed. When Babaji opened his eyes and said in his sweet voice, 'Children, as you know, I've come here today to make two lovers of freedom one,' the garden erupted in passionate slogans.

Nigar, in her bridal clothes, sat on one end of the stage with her head lowered. She looked beautiful in her khadi tricolour sari. Babaji gestured to her to come over and sat her down next to Ghulam Ali. At this, more passionate slogans rang out. Ghulam Ali's face glowed more brightly than usual. I looked closely and saw that when he took the marriage documents from his friend and gave them to Babaji, his hands were trembling.

There was a maulvi on the stage as well. He read the Koranic verses that are usually read on these occasions. Babaji closed his eyes. Once the marriage rites were complete, Babaji blessed the couple in his distinct way. And when dried dates were showered on the stage, he jumped at them like a child, collecting a few to keep next to him.

A Hindu girlfriend of Nigar's, smiling shyly, gave Ghulam Ali a little box and said something to him. Ghulam Ali opened the little box and marked Nigar's forehead with a streak of sindoor. Jallianwala Bagh once again thundered with applause. Babaji rose to address this clamour. The crowd immediately fell silent.

The pleasant scent of raat ki rani and jasmine floated through the mild evening air. It was a beautiful evening. Babaji's voice seemed sweeter still. After expressing his heartfelt joy at Ghulam Ali and Nigar's marriage, he said, 'These children will now serve their country and community with greater strength and purity. Because the true purpose of marriage is the pure friendship between a man and a woman. By being joined in friendship, Ghulam Ali and Nigar, together, can strive for freedom. In Europe, there are many such marriages whose objective is friendship and friendship alone. People such as these who remove lust from their lives are worthy of our respect.'

Babaji spoke at length about his convictions on marriage. His belief was that the real happiness of marriage could only be attained when the relations between a man and a woman were not physical. He didn't set nearly the same store by the sexual relationship between a man and a woman as society did. Thousands ate to satisfy their palate, but that didn't mean that doing so was a human obligation. Far fewer ate only to stay alive. But in reality, it was these few who knew the correct principles behind eating and drinking. Similarly, those who married so that they might know the higher sentiments of marriage, and realise its full purity, were the ones who would know the true joy of conjugal life.

Babaji explained the principles behind his convictions with a delicacy and subtlety that left the listener feeling that the doors to an entirely new world had opened for him. I myself found it very affecting. Ghulam Ali, who sat in front of me, seemed to drink in every word of his speech. When Babaji finished speaking, he said something to Nigar. After this, he rose and in a trembling voice announced: 'Mine and Nigar's marriage will be such an honourable marriage. Until the time when India attains its independence, mine and Nigar's relationship will be no more than a friendship.'

The still air of Jallianwala Bagh broke with the thunder of applause. Shahzada Ghulam Ali became emotional. His fair Kashmiri face filled with colour. In a surge of feeling he turned to Nigar and addressed her in a loud voice: 'Nigar! Are you willing to mother a slave child? Would that please you?'

Nigar, already unsettled, in part from becoming so recently married, and in part from hearing Babaji's speech, became still more perturbed when she heard this bolt from the blue. She was only able to say, 'Sorry? No, no, of course not.'

The crowd applauded again and Ghulam Ali became still more emotional. He was so overjoyed at having saved Nigar from the shame of mothering slave children that he strayed from the subject at hand and launched into a tirade on attaining independence. For more than an hour, he spoke in a voice filled with emotion. Then, all of a sudden, his gaze fell on Nigar, and for some reason, his charge drained out of him. Like a drunk man forking out note after note and finding his wallet suddenly empty, Ghulam Ali found his power of speech exhausted. It left him in some turmoil, but then he looked immediately at Babaji, and lowering his head in reverence, said, 'Babaji, we both ask your blessings that we may remain steadfast

115

in the oath we have taken tonight.'

The next day, at six in the morning, Ghulam Ali was arrested because in the speech he made after taking his oath, he had also threatened to overthrow the British government.

A few days after his arrest, Ghulam Ali was sentenced to eight months in prison and sent to Multan jail. He was Amritsar's forty first dictator and perhaps its forty thousand and first political prisoner. Forty thousand, as far as I can remember, was what the newspapers were quoting as the number arrested in the movement. The general view was that independence was now just a few steps away. But it had been the foreign politicians who had allowed the milk of this movement to reach its boiling point. And when they found they couldn't come to an agreement with the major Indian leaders, it turned quickly to cold lassi.

When the zealots were released from jail, they were forced to put the hardships of prison behind them, and set to work repairing their damaged businesses. Shahzada Ghulam Ali was released after only seven months. Though their former passion had fizzled out, people still gathered at Amritsar station to welcome him back. There were three or four dinners and meetings in his honour. I was present at all of them, but these gatherings were totally insipid. A strange fatigue prevailed, as if a man in the middle of a long distance run had suddenly been told, 'Stop, this race has to be run again.' And now, after catching their breath a while, it was as if the runners were reluctantly making their way back to the starting line.

Many years passed. That joyless fatigue didn't leave India. In my own world, many big and small revolutions occurred: my facial hair grew; I was admitted to college; I failed the FA examinations twice; my father died; I wandered about in search of employment. I was employed as a translator in a third rate newspaper. When I tired of this, I thought again of education. I was admitted to Aligarh University, but became a TB patient within only three months and went off to wander the Kashmiri countryside. Returning, I made for Bombay. Here, I saw three Hindu–Muslim riots in two years. When my nerves played up again, I went to Delhi. Compared to Bombay, I found everything there slowpaced. If there was movement here, it felt somehow effete. I felt Bombay was better. What did it matter that my next door neighbour didn't even find the time to ask me my name? Besides, all kinds of sicknesses grew in places where people have too much time on their hands. And so after two cold years spent in Delhi, I went back to ever-moving Bombay.

It had been some eight years since I had left home. I had had no news of friends or acquaintances, knew nothing of what state Amritsar's streets and alleys were in. I had written no letters, kept up no correspondence. Truth be told, in those eight years, I had become somewhat uncaring of my future and so, didn't dwell too long on the past. What was the point of accounting for what had been spent eight years before? After all, in life the pennies that are important are the ones you want to spend today or that might gain in value tomorrow.

I speak now of a time six years ago, when neither from life's rupees nor from silver ones, which carry the stamp of the emperor, had a penny been spent. But I couldn't have been too broke though because I was on my way at the time to Fort to buy myself an expensive pair of shoes. On one side of the Army and Navy store on Harbani Road, there was a shop whose display windows had attracted me for a while. My memory is weak and so I spent a considerable amount of time looking for the shop.

I had come to buy one pair of expensive shoes, but as is my tendency, I became absorbed by the displays in the other shops. I looked at a cigarette case in one shop, a pipe in another, and in this way, had wandered down the street until I found myself outside a small shoe shop. Standing in front of it, I thought, why not just buy my shoes here? The shopkeeper welcomed me and said, 'What are you looking for, sir?

I thought for a moment about what I wanted, and said, 'Yes, crepe rubber sole shoes.'

'We don't stock them here.'

The monsoon was approaching and so I thought that maybe I should buy some gumboots.

'In the next door shop,' the man replied. 'We don't stock any items made of rubber in this shop.'

'Why?' I asked absentmindedly.

'The owner's wish.'

Receiving this brief but faultless reply, I was about to leave the shop when I caught sight of a well dressed man standing on the pavement outside, carrying a child and buying oranges. I stepped outside and walked towards the fruit seller.

'Arre! Ghulam Ali!'

'Saadat!' he said, and with the child still in his arms, pressed me against his chest. The child didn't like this at all, and began to bawl. Ghulam Ali called over the man who a moment ago had told me that the shop didn't stock anything made of rubber, and handed him the child. 'Go and take him home,' he said, then turning to me: 'God, it's been a long time!'

I looked closely at his face. That playfulness, that rakish charm that had been his distinctive feature was gone. In place of the khadi clad young man, the fiery orator, there stood a domestic, ordinary sort of man. I remembered that last speech of his when he had set the still air of Jallianwala Bagh alight with the words, 'Nigar! Are you willing to mother a slave child? Would that please you?' Then, suddenly, I thought of the child he had been carrying a moment before. 'Whose child was that?' I asked. Without any hesitation, he replied, 'Mine. And there's one older than him as well. And you? How many have you produced?'

For an instant I felt that someone other than Ghulam Ali was speaking. All kinds of thoughts arose in my mind. Had Ghulam Ali completely forgotten his oath? Had he broken entirely with his political past? That passion to win India its independence, that temerity, where had it gone? What had happened to the boyish timbre of that voice? Where was Nigar? Had it pleased her in the end to mother two slave children? Perhaps she'd died. Perhaps Ghulam Ali had married again?

'What are you thinking? Speak to me, man. We're meeting after such a long time,' Ghulam Ali said,

119

slapping me hard on the shoulders.

I had fallen into silence. 'Yes,' I said with a start, still wondering how to initiate conversation. But without waiting for me, Ghulam Ali began, 'This shop is mine. I've been in Bombay for the past two years. The business is going really well. I end up saving some three, four hundred every month. What are you up to? I hear you've become a famous short story writer. Do you remember we once ran away from home and came here? But it's a strange thing, man, that Bombay and this Bombay seem so different. It feels as though that was smaller, and this bigger, somehow.'

In the meantime, a customer appeared, wanting tennis shoes. Ghulam told him, 'We don't stock anything made of rubber here. Try the shop next door.' When he'd gone, I said to Ghulam Ali, 'Why don't you stock anything made of rubber? In fact, I myself was just in there, looking for crepe rubber soled shoes.'

I'd asked the question casually, but Ghulam Ali's face all of a sudden became expressionless. In a low voice, he said no more than, 'I don't like it.'

'Don't like what?'

'Just that, rubber; things made from rubber.'

Saying this, he feigned a smile, but failing, cackled mirthlessly. 'I'll tell you,' he continued, 'I have a horror of it, but it has a very deep connection to my life.'

An expression of profound anxiety appeared on Ghulam Ali's face. His eyes, which still had some sparkle, dimmed for a moment, then brightened again. 'It was rubbish, man, that life. To tell the truth, Saadat, I've forgotten those days completely, when I had politics on the brain. For four or five years now, I've been living in great peace. I have a wife, kids… God's been kind.'

Moved still by God's kindness, Ghulam Ali began talking shop, about how much capital he'd begun with, his annual profit, how much he now had in the bank. I stopped him mid-sentence. 'You were saying that you had a horror of something and that it had a deep connection to your life.'

Once again his face became expressionless. He emitted a loud 'yes' and replied, 'There was a deep connection. Fortunately, there no longer is. But I'll have to tell you the whole story.'

In the meantime, his servant reappeared. Ghulam Ali put him in charge of the shop, and took me inside to his room. There, he sat me down and recounted at length the story of how his hatred of rubber had come to him.

'I don't need to tell you how my political life began, you know the story well. There's no need to tell you what my character was, you know that too. We were very alike in many ways. I mean to say that neither of our parents was in a position to say, "Our sons are perfect." I don't know why I'm telling you this, perhaps only to say, as you probably already know, that I was not a man of particularly firm character. But what I did have was the urge to do something. This is what drew me to politics. And I can say with all honesty that I wasn't a liar. I was prepared to give my life for my country. Even now, I'm prepared. But I've come to the conclusion, after much thought and consideration, that India's politics and its leaders are all, to a man, unready, just as I was. A wave rises, it is provoked, as far as I can tell, for waves don't rise by themselves, but perhaps I'm not explaining it very well... '

Ghulam Ali's thoughts were confused. I handed him a cigarette. He lit it, took three large drags and said, 'What do you think? Don't you feel that our every effort towards independence has been unnatural, not the effort I mean, but that its result has been unnatural every time? Why haven't we attained independence? Are we all in some way unmanly? No, we're all man enough. But we're in a climate in which our good, strong hand is not even allowed to reach near independence.'

'Do you mean to say that there's something standing in the way of us and independence?' I asked.

Ghulam Ali's eyes brightened. 'Absolutely. But this is not some solid wall, not a real barrier. It's a thin membrane: our own politics, our false existence, in which we not only deceive others, but ourselves as well.'

As before, his thoughts were scattered. My feeling was that he was trying to refresh in his mind, his own past experiences. He put out the cigarette and looking directly at me, said in a loud voice, 'Men must stay as they are. Is it necessary that someone doing good works should shave his head, don ascetic robes or rub ash over his body? You might say it's a matter of choice, of will. But I say that it's from this will itself, from this strange thing man possesses, that they become unmoored. The ones who rise above these things become oblivious to the natural weakness of men. They forget that their strength of character, their views, their principles, all blow away and are forgotten, and all that remain stamped on the minds of naive human beings are their shaved heads, their ash-covered bodies and their ascetic's clothes.' Ghulam Ali became still more impassioned. 'So many spiritual teachers have been born into the world. And though people have forgotten their teachings, their crucifixes, religious threads, beards, steel bangles and armpit hair endure. We, today, are more experienced than the people who lived here a thousand years before. And yet I can't understand how the spiritual leaders of today don't see that they are disfiguring people. I've felt the urge many times to start screaming, "For God's sake let men remain men! You've defaced them already, fine, now have mercy on their condition. While you're busy trying to make gods out of them, those poor wretches are losing whatever humanity they do have!" Saadat, I swear to God, this is my soul speaking, I'm telling you what I've experienced myself. If what I'm saying is wrong, then nothing is good or right. Two years, two full years, I spent wrestling with my mind. I fought with my heart, my conscience, my body, with every tiny hair on it, but each time I arrived at this conclusion: men must remain men. One in a thousand might kill his appetites, but if everyone was to kill their appetites, one has to ask: where is this mass killing getting us?' With this, he reached for another cigarette. He burned the matchstick to the end trying to light it, then gave his neck a light jerk. 'Nothing, Saadat! You don't know the spiritual and physical misery I've had to bear. But anyone who goes against nature is bound to know misery. That day, you'll recall, when in Jallianwala Bagh, I announced that Nigar and I would not give birth to slave children, I felt a strange kind of electric happiness. I felt, after this announcement, that my head had risen to touch the sky. But when I got out of jail, I began slowly to feel the pain of it... It was a source of torment to realise that I had paralysed a vital part of my soul and body. I took the most beautiful flower from the garden of my life and crushed it in my fingers. In the beginning, I derived a satisfaction from this realisation, knowing that I had done something others couldn't do. But slowly, reality, with all its bitterness, began to sink in.

'On returning from jail, I met Nigar. She had left the hospital and had gone to Babaji's ashram. I felt my eyes deceived me when I saw her changed complexion, her altered physical and mental state. Then, after living with her for a year, I discovered that her sorrow had been the same as mine. But neither she nor I were willing to express it. We were both enchained by our oath. Over the past year, our political passions had cooled. Khadi clothes and tricolour flags now no longer held the same appeal. If "Long Live the Revolution" was still to be heard, it no longer had the same ring to it. And in Jallianwala Bagh, not a single tent remained. The pegs of the old camps could still be seen in places, rooted in the ground. Political passion had drained out of everyone's blood. I, myself, spent much more time at home with my wife.' Once again, that wounded smile appeared on Ghulam Ali's lips and mid-sentence, he fell into silence. Not wanting to break his chain of thought, I said nothing.

A moment later, he wiped the sweat from his forehead and put out his cigarette. 'We were both in the grip of a strange curse. You know how much I love Nigar. But, I began thinking, what is the nature of this love? I can hold it and yet I won't allow it to reach its natural climax? Why am I afraid that I might commit a crime without meaning to? You know, I love Nigar's eyes. And so one morning when I was feeling very fine, not even fine, just normal really, as any man should be, I kissed them. I held her in my arms and a shudder went through me. It could be said that my soul broke free, spreading its wings, ready to make for the open sky, when I... when I seized it again and imprisoned it. Then for many days, I tried to convince myself that from this action of mine, from this heroic achievement, my soul knew a contentment that few others had known. But I failed to convince myself of this, and the knowledge of my failure, which I had tried to think of as a great success, made me—God is my witness—the most unhappy man in the world. But, as you know, men find their excuses. And, I, too, carved out a way.'

'We were rotting. Inside us, a kind of crust seemed to harden over our finer sensibilities. We became strangers to one another! I thought, after many days of consideration, that even if we stayed true to our oath, I mean that Nigar remained "unwilling to mother a slave child..."' As he said this, for the third time, that wounded smile appeared on Ghulam Ali's lips, but was changed instantly into an aimless cackle, in which his anguish was visible. Then, becoming serious, he said, 'A strange period began in our married life. Like a blind man granted a single eye, I was able, suddenly, to see. But after only a short while, this vision began to grow dim. In the beginning, we just thought that... ' Ghulam Ali seemed to search for the right words. 'In the beginning, we were satisfied. I mean, we had no idea that in a short while, we would find ourselves dissatisfied again, that one seeing eye would pressure the other to see as well. In that first stage, we felt ourselves becoming healthy. I could feel our vigour returning. Nigar's face had a flush to it. A sparkle showed in her eyes. The tension in my body melted away. But then slowly, we became like two rubber figurines. I felt it with greater force. You won't believe me, but I swear to God, when I'd pinch the flesh of my arms, it was exactly like rubber. It felt as though there were no veins inside. Nigar's condition, as far as I could tell, was not the same as mine. Her perspective was different: she wanted to be a mother. Whenever a child was born on our street, she would have to silently keep the longing she felt buried in her breast. In my case, I had no thought of children. So what if we didn't have any? There are many people in the world who are not blessed with children. Much better that I was true to my oath. This was comfort enough, but when fine strands of rubber began to spread like a web over my mind, my fears increased. I thought about it all the time and the result was that the texture of rubber was branded on my mind. I'd eat a bite of food and it would squelch below my teeth.' He said this and shuddered. 'It was an evil, disgusting thing. My fingers constantly felt soapy. I began to hate myself. It felt as though all the juices of my soul had been squeezed out and only the husk remained. Spent... spent.' Ghulam began to laugh. 'Thank God that curse has passed, but Saadat, after what anguish! Life became like a shrivelled bit of skin; all its beautiful desires had died. Only the sense of touch had become unnaturally acute, not acute really, one dimensional: in wood, in glass, in metal, in paper and in stone, in everything, the dead, nauseating softness of rubber!!! This affliction only became more forceful whenever I tried to think of its cause. I could have lifted this curse with two fingers and cast it aside, but I lacked the courage. I was looking for a saviour. In this sea of distress, I floundered for anything with which I might reach the shore. For a long time, I thrashed around. And then, one morning, I was reading a religious book in the sun, not really reading, glancing through, when my eyes fell on a hadis. I leapt up with happiness. My saviour was there in front of me. I read those lines again and again. My barren life was fertile once more. It was written that after marriage it is obligatory for husband and wife to produce a child. It was only lawful to prevent its birth if the mother's life was endangered as a result. And so, with two fingers, I lifted this curse and cast it aside.'

Saying this, he smiled like a child. I also smiled because he'd lifted the cigarette butt with two fingers and flicked it to one side as if it was something vile. Then, his smile vanished and he became serious. 'I know, Saadat,' he said, 'that what I've told you right now, you're going to turn into a story. But listen, don't mock me in it. I swear to you, whatever I've told you is exactly what I experienced. I won't argue with you on this subject, but what I have learned is that to go against nature is in no way, under no circumstances, bravery. It's no achievement to kill yourself through abstinence, or to endure it. To dig your grave and get in it, holding your breath for days, to sleep for months on beds of sharp nails, to keep one arm raised over your head for years so that it dries up and becomes like a piece of wood—stunts like these will bring neither God nor freedom. And from what I understand of it, the only reason India is still not free is that we've had too few leaders and too many stuntmen. What principles there are go against the nature of men. They've found a politics that stifles truth and goodness of character and it's this same politics that has made the struggle for independence so blinkered.'

Ghulam Ali was going to say more when his servant appeared. He carried Ghulam Ali's second child, perhaps. The boy held a bright balloon in his hand. Ghulam Ali reached adoringly for him. A noise like a firecracker going off was heard. The balloon exploded and the child was left holding a dangling string, attached to a little bit of rubber. Ghulam Ali snatched it with two fingers and threw it aside as though it was something truly repugnant.

Smell

Those same days of rain; outside the window, the peepal's leaves were washed in the same way. On the teak spring bed, which had now been moved slightly away from the window, a Marathi girl clung to Randhir.

Outside the window, the peepal's leaves like long earrings, clattered in the pale darkness. The Marathi girl, like a shudder herself, clung to Randhir. It had been nearly evening, when after spending the day reading the news and advertisements in an English newspaper, he had stepped onto the balcony for some air. It was there that he saw her, a worker perhaps in the nearby rope factory, taking shelter under a tamarind tree. He drew her attention by clearing his throat and gestured to her to come upstairs.

He'd been feeling very lonely for many days. Because of the war, virtually all Bombay's Christian girls, inexpensive in the past, had joined the Women's Auxiliary Force. Some of them had opened dancing schools in the vicinity of Fort where only white soldiers were allowed entry. This was the cause of Randhir's deep depression: on one hand Christian girls becoming scarce; on the other, Randhir, far more refined, educated, healthy and handsome than the white soldiers, finding the doors of the dancing bars closed to him because the colour of his skin was not white.

Before the war, Randhir had had sexual relations with many Christian girls near Nagpara and the Taj Hotel. He knew the nature of these relationships. He knew far better than those Christian mongrels that the girls carried on romances purely for the sake of fashion, but would in the end invariably marry some asshole.

After all it was only to take revenge on Hazel that he had gestured to the Marathi girl to come upstairs. Hazel lived in the flat below. Every morning she wore her uniform, tipped her khaki cap to one side over her short hair, and stepped out onto the pavement as if expecting the other pedestrians to lay themselves down like a rug at her feet. Randhir wondered why he was so drawn to these Christian girls. There was no doubt that they well displayed those parts of their body that were worth displaying; they discussed the irregularities of their period without the slightest hesitation; they told stories of old lovers; and when they heard dancing music, they began to shake a leg... that was all fine, but surely any woman could possess these qualities.

Randhir didn't think he would sleep with the Marathi girl when he had gestured to her to come upstairs. But a few moments later, after seeing her wet clothes and thinking, 'I hope the poor thing doesn't get pneumonia', he said, 'Take these clothes off or you'll catch a cold.'

She understood his meaning because the veins in her eyes reddened and seemed to swim. But when Randhir took out his white dhoti and handed it to her, she thought it over and opened her kashta*, now more visibly dirty for being wet. She put it to one side and hurriedly wrapped the dhoti round her thighs. She tried taking off her tight blouse, but its ends were tied in a knot that was buried in her shallow, dirty cleavage.

---

* A style of draping a sari—common among the Brahmin women especially in Maharashtra, Karnataka, Andhra Pradesh and Tamil Nadu—so that the sari's center is placed neatly at the back of the waist and the ends are tied securely in the front, with two ends wrapped around the legs.

She tried at length, with the help of her worn down nails, to open the blouse's knot, but it had become tough with rain. Tiring at last, she gave up, saying something to Randhir in Marathi, the meaning of which was: 'What am I to do? It won't open.'

Randhir sat down beside her and began opening the knot. But he soon tired of it too, and taking one end of the blouse in each hand, he pulled. The knot slipped; Randhir's hands flew everywhere; two throbbing breasts came into view. Randhir felt for a moment that his own hands, like those of some expert potter, had fashioned two cups of soft, kneaded clay on this Marathi girl's chest.

Her breasts had the same half-ripened, juice-filled quality, the same appeal, the same warm coolness that is found in the still-wet dishes that come freshly from the hands of a potter. Mixed into these youthful, unstained breasts was a strange shine. It was as if a layer of dim light under their dark, wheatish colour gave off this shine, a shine that was both present and not. The swell of her breasts had the aspect of clay lamps burning through murky water.

Those same days of rain. The peepal's leaves clattered outside the window. The Marathi girl's soaked clothes lay in a squalid heap on the floor; and she clung to Randhir. The warmth of her naked and dirty body produced the same sensation in him as that of bathing in bitter winter in a barber's grimy, but warm hamam.

All night she clung to Randhir. The two became fused to one another. No more than two words passed between them, but everything that needed to be said was communicated through their lips, breath and hands.

All night, Randhir's hands ran as lightly as air over the Marathi girl's breasts. Her tiny nipples and the fat bumps that were spread in a black circle round them would awaken with the sensation, producing in her body such a frisson that Randhir himself was left trembling.

He had known this trembling many times before; he was well-acquainted with its pleasure. He had passed nights like this before, pressing his chest against the soft and firm breasts of many girls. He had slept with girls who were totally unversed and wrapped themselves around him, telling him everything about their homes that should never be told to a stranger. He'd had sexual relations with girls who would do all the hard work themselves and never give him an ounce of trouble. But this Marathi girl who had stood drenched under the tamarind tree, and to whom he had gestured to come upstairs, was different.

Randhir inhaled a strange smell coming from her body all night; it was at once foul and sweet-smelling, and he drank it in. From her armpits, her breasts, her hair, her back—from everywhere; it became part of every breath Randhir took. All night he thought, this Marathi girl despite being so close to me would not be nearly so close if it were not for this smell coming from her naked body. It had trickled into each groove of his mind, inhabiting his old and new thoughts.

The smell soldered Randhir and this girl together for that night. They both entered each other. They descended to great depths, became one, pure pinnacle of human bliss, a bliss that despite being temporary is permanent, despite being airborne is immobile and immovable. The two had become like a bird that after soaring into the blues of the sky comes to seem motionless.

Randhir understood the smell that came from every pore of this Marathi girl, but he was unable to compare it to anything, like with the smell that comes from water sprinkled on mud. But no, that smell was different; in this, there was nothing of the falsity of lavender and attar; it was utterly real, like the unifying relations between men and women, real and immemorial.

Randhir detested the smell of sweat. After bathing, he usually put scented powder in his armpits and other areas; or some other concoction that suppressed the smell of sweat. What surprised him now was that he felt no revulsion at kissing this Marathi girl's hairy armpits; instead he felt a strange kind of pleasure. Her soft armpit hair had become moist with sweat. The smell that came from them, though comprehensible on so many levels, was in the end incomprehensible. Randhir felt he knew it, recognised it, even understood its meaning, but couldn't make anyone else understand.

Those same days of rain. He looked out of the same window to see the clattering peepal's leaves washed in the rain. Their sound, and the rustle of the wind, seemed to coalesce. It was dark, but light lay buried in the darkness as though a bit of starlight had made its way down with the raindrops. Those days of rain, when in Randhir's room, there had been only a single teak bed. Now there was another one next to it; and in the corner, a new dressing table. Those same days of rain, that same season, a little starlight making its way down with the raindrops. But the air now was infused with scent of henna.

133

The other bed was empty. In the bed on which Randhir lay sideways, watching the play of raindrops on the peepal leaves outside, a fair-skinned woman, after trying vainly to conceal her naked upper body with her arms, had fallen asleep. Her red silk salwar lay on the other bed; one tassel from its deep red drawstring hung down. Her other clothes also lay on the bed; her bra, her underpants, her kameez with its gold flowers, her dupatta—all red, astonishingly red. They were imbued with the powerful scent of henna. Little flecks of glitter collected like dust in the girl's hair. On her face, glitter, rouge and lipstick had come together to produce a strange colour, faded and lifeless. Her bra strap had left stains on her white chest.

Her breasts were milky white, but with a hint of blue. Her armpits were shaved, making them seem dusted with kohl. Randhir had looked at this girl many times and thought, 'Isn't it as if I've just torn open a wooden carton and taken her out, like a stack of books or china dishes. She even has marks and scratches like those on books and china.'

Randhir had opened her bra's tight, close-fitting straps; its impression could be seen in the soft flesh on her back and chest. There was also a stain on her waist from her tightly tied drawstring. Her heavy necklace, with its sharp points, had left indentations on her chest, as if nails had dug forcefully at it. Those same days of rain. The raindrops falling on the peepal's smooth, soft leaves, making the same sound Randhir had heard throughout that night. The weather was perfect; a cool breeze blew; but the powerful scent of henna flowers was mixed into it.

Randhir's hands ran like air over this pale, fair-skinned girl's milky white breasts. His fingers set loose a shiver through her soft body. When he pressed his chest against hers, he could hear the sound of every chord that had been struck in this girl. But where was that cry, the cry that he had inhaled in the smell of that Marathi girl, the cry that was infinitely more comprehensible than that of a child thirsty for milk, the cry that after exceeding the limits of the voice (from which it broke), became inaudible?

Randhir was looking out of the window grilles. The peepal's leaves clattered very near him, but he was trying to look much further than that, to where a strange dim light was visible through murky clouds, a light like the one he had seen in the Marathi girl's breasts, a light, which like the contents of a secret was both hidden and evident.

In Randhir's arms, lay a fair-skinned girl whose body was soft like dough mixed with milk and butter; from her sleeping body came the now tired scent of henna; to Randhir, it was as unpleasant as a man's last breath, and sour, like a belch. Discoloured. Sad. Joyless.

Randhir looked at the girl who lay in his arms as one looks at curdled milk, with its lifeless white lumps afloat in pallid water. In the same way, this girl's womanliness left him cold. His mind and body were still consumed by the smell that came naturally from the Marathi girl; the smell that was many times more subtle and pleasurable than that of henna; that he had not been afraid to inhale, that had entered him of its own accord and realised its true purpose.

Randhir made one last effort to touch this girl's milky white body. But he felt no trembling. His brand new wife

135

who was the daughter of a first class magistrate, who had attained a BA, who was the heartthrob of so many boys in her college did not quicken his pulse. In the deathly scent of henna, he searched for that smell that in those same days of rain, when in an open window the peepal's leaves were washed, he had inhaled from the dirty body of a Marathi girl.

A note on the author

Saadat Hasan Manto has been called the greatest short story writer of the Indian subcontinent. He was born in 1912 in Punjab and went on to become a radio and film scriptwriter, journalist and short story writer. His stories were highly controversial and he was tried for obscenity six times during his career. After Partition, Manto moved to Lahore with his wife and three daughters. He died there in 1955.

A note on the translator

Aatish Taseer was born in 1980 and educated at Amherst College. He has worked as a reporter for *Time* magazine and is the author of *Stranger to History*, which will be published next year. He divides his time between London and Delhi.

A note on the type

This book was set in Adobe Caslon, a variant of Caslon designed by Carol Twombly. Caslon was originally designed and engraved by William Caslon of William Caslon & Son, Letter-Founders, in London, and first released in 1722. Caslon's types were based on seventeenth century Dutch old style designs and met with instant success, becoming popular throughout Europe and the American colonies. For her revival of the typeface, Twombly studied specimen pages printed between 1734 and 1770.